Dirty Sexy Sinner

NEW YORK TIMES BESTSELLING AUTHORS

Carly Phillips

Erika Wilde

Copyright © Karen Drogin 2016 and © Janelle Denison 2016
Print Edition
CP Publishing 2016

Cover photo: Sara Eirew
Design: Maria @SteamyDesigns

"The love story Phillips and Wilde crafted was rare, dipped in a reality so natural and organic it held my heart from the very first page."
~ Audrey Carlan, #1 New York Times Bestselling Author

New York Times bestselling authors Carly Phillips and Erika Wilde bring you a dirty, sexy, smoking hot series featuring four bad boy brothers bonded by shocking secrets and their damaged past. Sinful, addicting, and unapologetically alpha, these men are every woman's erotic daydream … And your ultimate dirty fantasy.

Are you ready to get in bed with a SINNER?

After a lifetime of lies, deceit and betrayal, Jackson Stone isn't a man who trusts easily—with women being at the top of the list. Now he's all about control in every aspect of his life. Especially between the sheets. Hot, mutual pleasure with a woman? No problem, as long as he's in charge. But there's something different about sexy bartender Tara Kent that he finds irresistible, in bed and out. Something that has him willing to compromise his principles and bend his rules. Let the sinning begin . . .

* * *

Chapter One

J ACKSON STONE'S ENTIRE life had been a goddamn lie, and in a matter of minutes, he was about
to confront the truth, along with the fact that he had
three brothers he hadn't even known existed until two
weeks ago. He was still dealing with, and sorting
through, the shock of learning the details surrounding
his birth and illegal adoption, and he had no idea if his
three siblings—one of which was his twin—were even
aware of *his* existence.

He was about to find out, but ultimately it didn't
matter if they knew of him or not, because facing his
brothers was something he had to do. If anything,
Jackson hoped meeting them gave him some kind of
closure. He'd spent the past thirty-two years feeling
like an outsider in his own family and wondering why
his father—or rather, the man who'd raised him—had
always favored his younger son while blatantly ignoring any attempt Jackson had made to win Paul Stone's

affection and approval.

But now that Jackson had discovered the truth about where he'd come from, his father's rejection made so much more sense to him. Unfortunately, his entire childhood had been a mind-fuck, and nothing had been as it seemed. Even as an adult, the emotional damage his father had inflicted during those younger, formative years, combined with his ex-wife's betrayal, made it difficult for Jackson to let anyone close. The few people he trusted implicitly, he could count on one hand, and he doubted that would change anytime soon.

He pushed those thoughts from his mind and rolled his tense shoulders just as the navigation system announced that he'd arrived at his destination—a bar named Kincaid's that was located in a less-than-desirable neighborhood in Chicago. He turned his Porsche into the parking area behind the building, his gleaming dark gray sports car glaringly out of place next to the few older vehicles in the lot.

Not wanting to risk getting the paint scratched or dinged, he parked his car in the farthest row, away from everyone else. The 911 Carrera was his baby, a gift to himself when he'd made partner at Schmidt and Kramer, the architect firm where he'd worked the past eleven years. Yeah, he was a bit obsessive about keeping the Porsche in pristine condition, but considering he'd worked his ass off to be able to afford such an indulgence, he didn't mind going out of his way to protect his investment.

Sliding out of the low-slung car, he straightened to his full height and engaged the alarm system, then glanced at his watch. It was three thirty in the afternoon, a half hour before the establishment opened. He was hoping that by arriving early he'd be able to catch Clay, the brother who owned the place, *and his twin*, before the bar started letting customers in for the evening.

As he approached the old, dated building, out of habit he found himself eyeing the place from an architect's perspective. He was used to working on urban designs, corporate buildings, and sophisticated and luxurious structures, but the modest bar that had probably been built in the 1980s fit the blue-collar neighborhood. The place looked clean and well taken care of and appeared as though it had been recently treated with new wood trim and a fresh coat of paint.

He didn't know much about the Kincaid brothers, just the basic information he'd enlisted a private investigator to provide so he had an initial point of contact and could introduce himself to the men. Names, ages, marital status, and place of business was what Jackson had asked for, and that's all he'd been given. The PI had offered to deliver an in-depth background report on all three men, but Jackson had declined. He wasn't looking to blatantly invade their privacy. If the situation were reversed, he wouldn't appreciate his entire life and past being scrutinized by a virtual stranger or conclusions made about his character based on information provided by a third party.

He reached the front entrance to the bar. The hours of operation stated they didn't open until four, but figuring the employees arrived earlier, he pulled on the iron handle anyway. His nerves ratcheted up a notch as the door opened, bringing him one step closer to meeting his brothers. Uncertainty and anticipation mingled inside him as he entered the vacant lobby.

He was a confident, successful, and respected businessman, but there was no way of knowing what kind of reception he was about to receive. His stomach pitched at the possibility that his siblings might not want to have anything to do with him, or make it clear that he didn't belong.

Yeah, the fucking story of my life, Jackson thought as he forcibly shook off the mental and physical anxiety trying to take hold. Exhaling a deep breath, he moved toward the sounds coming from the main bar, where the lighting was dimmed. He caught sight of a young woman setting out a garnish tray at the service area, who absently glanced his way as soon as he came into sight, immediately pegging him as a customer.

"I'm sorry," she said, giving him an apologetic smile as she added a stack of napkins to the counter. "But we don't open until four . . ."

As he stood there, her gaze skimmed over his Armani suit and up to his face. A look of utter confusion creased her brows, and he was pretty sure he knew why. Her boss and his twin, Clay Kincaid, obviously wasn't a business suit kind of guy, and that was throwing her off, along with similarities Jackson must share with his brother. With a tilt of her head, she took in his short cropped hair and studied his features, and when she finally met his gaze, he couldn't hold back the amused smile that tugged up the corners of his lips.

Her perplexed expression turned to one of unmitigated shock as she realized he wasn't her employer. Exotic eyes, a stunning shade of bright azure blue, widened, and she shook her head wildly in disbelief, causing long, dark strands of her silky-looking hair to brush back and forth across her shoulders.

"You're not Clay," she blurted out.

"No, I'm not," he confirmed in a low, husky voice as he caught sight of a small diamond piercing above her sensual upper lip. "I'm his twin brother, Jackson Stone."

"His twin," she repeated, still staring at him, her tone soft with awe as her disbelief gradually morphed into curious bewilderment, along with a noticeable flicker of fascination. "Holy . . . shit. Clay has a fucking twin."

He chuckled, enjoying her unfiltered response. Found it refreshing, actually. He was used to polite, sophisticated women. The kind who tended to be sweet, prim, and proper in his presence and a catty bitch behind his back. This beauty in front of him was edgy and direct, and damn if he didn't find the straightforward combination sexy as fuck.

"This is . . . crazy," she said, still trying to process everything about him and the situation. "Does Clay know you were stopping by?"

He heard the cautious, slightly protective note to her voice that told him just how loyal this woman was to her boss and decided to be completely honest with her. "I'm pretty sure he doesn't even know I exist."

Questions filled her expressive blue eyes as he moved even closer to her side of the bar, but she didn't ask any of them, which he appreciated.

"Is he here, by chance?" Jackson asked hopefully.

"No. Wednesday nights are pretty slow." She was still staring at him, and an undeniable—and mutual—awareness simmered between them. "Most likely, he's at home with his wife."

His brothers' marital statuses had been included in his condensed background report, so Jackson was at least familiar with their significant others. Clay, owner of Kincaid's, was married to Samantha. Mason, owner of Inked, a tattoo shop, was married to Katrina. And Levi, the youngest brother, who was a cop for Chicago PD, had recently become engaged to a woman named Sarah.

"Is there a way I can get ahold of him?" Now that Jackson was finally here, he didn't want to drag this first meeting out any longer than necessary. The proverbial cat was out of the bag, and he also didn't want to give any of the Kincaid brothers a reason to say no to meeting him.

She bit that lush bottom lip of hers, clearly considering his request while he contemplated her seductive mouth in general and the sinful things he'd like to do to it. But once again, Jackson instinctively knew her loyalty to Clay would win out and she wouldn't be doing anything to or with him. Not until Clay had given Jackson his stamp of approval. As frustrating as that was, he couldn't help but respect her for being so trustworthy.

"You seem like a really nice guy, Jackson," she finally said earnestly. "I won't give out Clay's personal information, but I can do one of two things for you. I can take your information and pass it along to Clay, or I can call him now and see if he's able to come down to the bar and meet you."

Grateful that she hadn't completely shut him down, he pushed his hands into the front pockets of his pants and graced her with one of his charming grins. "I'll take option number two, please."

She returned his smile before pulling her cell phone from the back pocket of her jeans. She pressed a few buttons on the screen of her phone, then held it up to her ear while half turning away from him, so that her face was averted, which he didn't mind one damn bit considering the sexy view she'd just presented him with. While she waited for someone to answer her call, his gaze shamelessly skimmed down the side profile of her made-for-sin body, taking in her full, high breasts beneath the Kincaid's T-shirt she wore and the sweet curve of her ass outlined in her formfitting jeans.

His eyes remained right there as a lustful heat

coursed through his veins, turning up the temperature of his blood a few degrees. As he was a man who appreciated a toned and firm backside on a woman, hers teased him with the mental image of grabbing her ass while he pulled her hips toward his or smacking that softly rounded flesh with the palm of one hand while his other one fisted all that beautiful, long hair tight between his fingers as he aligned himself behind her.

He didn't even try and waylay the twitch of his dick as those dirty thoughts filled his mind. No, he actually welcomed his body's reaction to her. It had been too fucking long since any woman had piqued his interest or stimulated his cock. In just a matter of minutes, she'd managed both and he was definitely intrigued.

"Hey, hi, Clay, it's Tara," she finally said, trying to sound casual as she greeted her boss on the phone while also making Jackson privy to her name. "No, everything is just fine," she rushed to assure him while casting a surreptitious glance back at him. "I'm calling because someone is at the bar to see you . . . and he wants it to be a surprise."

Jackson hadn't told her that, but he assumed she didn't want to announce to Clay over the phone that he had a long-lost twin. Her delicate way of handling his impromptu visit was yet another thing he was grateful for, and a part of him was sorry for putting her in the middle of the situation.

As she listened to whatever Clay was saying to her

in response, she rolled her eyes at Jackson, giving him the impression that Clay was trying to wheedle more information out of her. Behind him, he could hear people walking by . . . most likely employees getting ready for their shift, but they paid him no attention. Clearly, he didn't resemble Clay from the back view, at least not dressed in an expensive suit.

"I know I'm being cryptic, but trust me, Clay," she said persuasively. "You just need to come down to the bar and see for yourself. In fact, if Mason and Levi can join you, that would be even better."

Meeting all three of his brothers at once was Jackson's preference, too.

She went quiet while Clay talked another few seconds, then she finally said, "Okay, thank you." Relief filled her tone. "I'll see you in about half an hour."

With a press of her finger, she disconnected the call, her expression conflicted when she turned fully toward Jackson again. "Clay sounded so suspicious on the phone," she said with a grimace as she dragged her fingers through her hair. "God, he's going to kill me for not giving him a heads-up about you."

"It's better this way," he said, hoping to reassure her.

She nodded in understanding. "I know. That's why I didn't break the news to him that he had a twin." She released a soft little laugh. "I mean, how do you explain something like that on the phone? It's something Clay has to see for himself to believe it, and I didn't want to give him the next half hour to drive himself nuts thinking about the hows and whys of your existence. That's your story to tell."

Yes, it was, and even he had to admit that the tale was one helluva story that had taken even him time to digest and accept. "Thank you, Tara."

She gave him a wry look that was tinged with humor. "You can thank me by giving me a job at whatever fancy place you work at once Clay fires me for keeping you a secret."

He chuckled. "If that happens, I promise I'll make you my personal assistant." As soon as the words left his mouth, his filthy mind imagined all the *personal* things she could do for him, and it had nothing to do with paperwork or fielding phone calls. No, it involved her servicing him in a whole different way.

She raised a perfectly arched brow, completely unaware of the direction his thoughts had just traveled. "I'm going to hold you to that, Mr. Stone."

Her light, feisty personality had the tension in his shoulders ebbing, and for the first time since walking into the bar, he began to relax. Tara was like a breath of fresh air compared to how stifled and guarded he felt around most of the women he'd casually dated since his divorce. There were no expectations or pretenses with her and no reason for her to try and impress him.

A perky blonde with a bounce in her step walked around Jackson and behind the bar. She was wearing the same T-shirt-and-jeans uniform as Tara, and she gave him a brief glance—the physical differences between him and Clay not yet registering.

"Hey, Clay, what are you doing here all dressed up in a suit? Is Samantha dragging you off to somewhere classier than this joint?" she teased over her shoulder as she put her purse into a cupboard.

Tara's eyes glimmered with mirth. "Take another look, Amanda. That's not Clay. It's his twin, Jackson."

"Ha ha," Amanda responded drolly as she shifted her gaze back to him, clearly taking Tara's comment as a joke.

The other woman studied Jackson for a casual moment, focusing on his facial features and the cut of his hair. It was comical to watch that shift from *of course this is my boss, Clay* to that moment when she realized that Tara hadn't been yanking her chain after all.

Amanda's jaw literally dropped open, then snapped shut again. "Clay has a freakin' twin?" she exclaimed, loud enough that a few other employees in the place glanced his way curiously, as well.

Tara laughed. "That's what I just told you."

The initial nonchalance in Amanda's gaze dissipated as she assessed Jackson through a new, unfiltered perspective—slowly and appreciatively. "Jesus, and I thought Clay was hot," she murmured flirtatiously.

He didn't miss the subtle come-on in her words, but he wasn't the least bit tempted. Now, if it had been Tara issuing the invitation, he would have seriously considered his options.

As if sensing the suddenly awkward vibe in the air,

Tara stepped in front of Amanda and changed the subject. "Why don't you take a seat at the far end of the bar while you wait for the guys to get here?" she suggested to him.

"Where I'll be less distracting?" he asked with a half grin as he walked in that direction, away from the main traffic area and the other employees arriving for their shifts.

She gave him a sassy little smirk. "Yeah, that, too."

He slid onto the last cushioned stool at the bar, and she followed him from the other side of the counter. The lighting at this end was more muted, which made it feel more private. At least for now.

She set a cocktail napkin in front of him. "Can I get you anything to drink?"

He glanced at the selection of premium liquor on the top shelf behind the bar and was surprised that he found the high-end brand he was searching for. "I'll take the Bushmills 21 neat."

She tipped her head inquisitively, bringing his attention once again to the small, sexy diamond stud winking at him from her upper lip. "We don't get many requests for the Bushmills, considering most of our clientele in this area tend to order the cheap and dirty drinks, but I should have guessed a sophisticated guy like you would go right for the most expensive brand of liquor we've got in the place."

Standing on the tips of her toes, she reached up to grab the distinctive bottle of alcohol, and his gaze automatically gravitated to the enticing swells of her ass once again. Fuck, she was hot. He lingered longer than he'd intended on what was quickly becoming his favorite view, and when she turned back around, he knew he'd been caught in the act. And he was now looking at that sweet spot at the juncture of her slender thighs—an equally captivating sight that had his body humming with heated awareness.

There was no denying what he'd been staring at, and without an ounce of remorse, he lifted his eyes back up to hers. Yep, he'd been busted, but the glimpse of amusement he saw dancing in those stunning blue irises and the arousing-as-hell flush on her cheeks told him that she hadn't been the least bit offended by his perusal of her ass.

No, she certainly wasn't shying away from the attraction simmering between them, nor was she playing hard to get like other women he'd dated—female games that bored him or made him suspicious of their motives. He liked flirting with Tara. Liked that there were no contrived pretenses in their interactions, and he in turn could just be himself, as well.

"If you don't sell a lot of this particular brand, why carry it?" he asked casually as she poured his drink with a quick, deft hand. From a business perspective, it seemed like a waste of space and money to him.

"Because every so often, Clay or Mason will indulge in their favorite whiskey, and that would be the Bushmills 21." She placed the lowball glass filled with the amber liquid on the napkin in front of him. "That's the only reason it's on the shelf. Just goes to show that you really are Clay's twin."

He chuckled lightly. "Just in case my looks didn't convince you?"

That sweet, addictive laugh escaped her lips once again. "You're the spitting image of your brother, but I'm pretty sure the two of you couldn't be more different in most other ways."

"Such as?" he wanted to know.

"Well, for one thing, the only time I've ever seen Clay in a suit was when he got married, and you look like you wear one on a daily basis." Her gaze took in his facial features, then his hair. "I'm guessing you live in the city and have some kind of corporate career, while Clay hates downtown Chicago and is definitely not the kind of guy to work a nine-to-five shift. I'm guessing your general lifestyles are pretty opposite."

He didn't get the impression that she was judging him in any way, and quite honestly, her speculation about him was pretty spot on based on his outer appearance. But Jackson hadn't grown up in the lap of luxury as she probably assumed, nor had there been any emotional support that might have helped guide him toward the kind of future most parents would want for their kid.

Far from it. Jackson had been motivated to build a successful life for himself based on his anger and resentment toward the man he'd believed was his father but who had never treated him like a son. He'd grown up feeling worthless and insignificant compared to his younger brother, and not knowing the *why* of his father's actions had spawned all sorts of insecurities. Doubting himself, and feeling like he didn't belong no matter how hard he tried to please his father, had been the most painful.

Once he'd turned eighteen and left home, Jackson had achieved every single goal he'd set for himself—starting with college and the school loans he'd paid for himself over the years, through an internship at a prestigious architectural firm, to finally being hired on in a full-time position with Schmidt and Kramer and becoming partner, to making a respectable six-figure salary, with impressive quarterly bonuses. He'd invested his money well and had a solid seven figures to his name.

From anyone on the outside looking in, it appeared that he'd built a fucking fantastic life for himself, and he had. But everything he'd accomplished and obtained had never filled that empty hole inside of him. His marriage certainly hadn't lived up to his expectations of what he thought would bring him ultimate happiness. He wondered if anything ever would.

Tara had gone back to prepping the bar while he'd been lost in his thoughts, and he sipped his whiskey as he watched her move with purpose as she stocked glasses, replaced liquor bottles, and organized things to her liking. Other staff members were milling about, some of whom were blatantly staring at him with shock as they glanced his way. Obviously, Amanda, the other bar waitress, had let staff members in on the fact that Clay had a twin, and they wanted to see him for themselves.

After a short while, Tara came back to his end of the bar to check on him. "You doing okay down here? Would you like another drink?"

He swirled the last bit of liquor in his glass and shook his head. "No, I'm good. Thanks." The one drink had been just enough to somewhat relax him, though he was still a bit anxious about meeting his siblings. He didn't think there was anything, legal anyway, that would quell that particular nervous anticipation thrumming through him.

Trying to tamp down his restlessness, he glanced at his watch. Twenty minutes had passed since she'd made the phone call to Clay. The place was still empty of customers since it was ten minutes until opening time. Tara didn't move away. Instead she started pushing bottles of beer into the ice bin on the other side of the counter where he was sitting, and he decided to take advantage of any knowledge she might want to share about the Kincaid brothers.

"So, what are the three of them like?" he asked before he changed his mind about prying. He wasn't asking for deep, personal secrets. He just wanted to know a bit about their personalities before he met them to put *him* more at ease. Yeah, he knew it was an unfair advantage to learn about his siblings before they even knew he existed, but it was three against one in the upcoming introduction, and he needed all the leverage he could get.

Tara glanced up at him, her eyes filled with emphatic kindness, as if she understood his concern about meeting the men he knew absolutely nothing about. "Well, the three of them are tight, and life for them hasn't always been easy," she said as she wiped her damp hands on a white terry towel. "In fact, they've gone through a lot of shit together since they were kids, so don't be too disappointed and don't take it personally if they're a bit distrusting when they first meet you."

He nodded. "I figured as much." Despite them sharing a birth mother, Jackson was still a stranger, after all. He wasn't expecting them to welcome him with open arms, but he hoped they would at least give him a chance to get to know the three of them better.

From his sitting position at the very end of the counter, he watched as a young couple entered the bar and took a seat at one of the round tables in the main area. They were the first customers of the evening, which meant Clay was that much closer to arriving. He finished off his Bushmills and pushed the glass away.

"Clay is a little rough around the edges," Tara went on as she tucked the towel into the waistband of her jeans. "But he's a really great guy once you get to know him. Around here, he has the nickname of Saint Clay because he's something of a do-gooder."

He rested his arms on the counter, his curiosity getting the best of him. "A do-gooder, huh?"

She picked up his empty glass and put it in the sink beneath the counter. "Yeah. He's someone who genuinely wants to help out other people because he knows what it's like to struggle. Most of us who work here were hired because we really needed the job for one reason or another."

The underlying gratitude toward her boss in her tone spoke volumes and hinted at Clay's influence in her life. "Including you?" he asked.

"Yeah, including me," she admitted softly.

He wondered about those shadows in her eyes, wanted to know where they'd come from and what she'd been through, but she quickly blinked them away before he could analyze those emotions any further.

"Clay's like a brother to me," she said with a shrug, her words helping to explain her loyalty to her boss. "Actually, all three of them are like family. They're very protective, but it's kind of nice knowing that someone has my back, and I always know that they'll be there for me if I need anything at all. That's just the kind of guys they are."

He didn't miss the fact that she said nothing of her own family. "And Mason? He owns a tattoo place, right?"

"Yeah. He's the hell-raiser out of the three. Smart mouth. Womanizer." She set a glass pitcher on the base of a blender, continuing her bar setup as she talked. "Well, he *was* a player until he finally came to his senses and realized that his best friend, Katrina, was the only woman for him. It's actually quite amusing to see him so mellow and wrapped around Katrina's finger."

The fondness in Tara's voice made Jackson smile.

"Then there's Levi, who couldn't be more different than his brothers," she continued, more animated now. "He's a police officer with Chicago PD. He's quiet and reserved but intense in his own way. He may not say much, but he doesn't miss a single damn thing going on around him."

All interesting facts about each brother that Jackson made a mental note of. He had a feeling all those details would come in handy very soon.

"Tara," a deep male voice called out from the other side of the bar. "Where's this person who's here to see us?"

The beautiful bartender standing across from Jackson had been so caught up in their conversation—hell, he'd been just as engaged—that her entire body visibly jolted in surprise when someone called her name. Before Jackson lifted his head to glance toward the entrance area behind her, Tara's big, wide eyes already told him who had arrived. *Clay.* And judging by the word *us* that he'd just used, he'd brought his brothers with him as she'd requested.

He exhaled a calming breath as Tara turned around and addressed the three men waiting to find out who their visitor was. She took a small step to the side, blocking their view of Jackson to give him another moment to collect his composure before they caught a glimpse of him. It also gave him the chance to slide off his stool and stand up so he was on an even playing field when he came face-to-face with his twin.

"He's down here, guys," she said, her voice steady

and even, but the way her fingers were twisting around the hand towel she'd tucked into her jeans gave her own nervousness away.

A handful of seconds later, the three men rounded the bar at the far end, and Clay came to an abrupt stop when he looked at Jackson's face, which was an exact reflection of his own. Just as suddenly, his brothers halted beside him as they realized the same thing. Hell, even Jackson was taken aback by the identical appearance of the man standing in front of *him*, and he'd had warning.

Physically, they were the same tall height, their bodies the same solid build. Both of them had dark brown hair, though Clay's was a bit longer and more disorderly than Jackson wore his. They possessed the same color eyes in a dark shade of brown flecked with gold, but it was their prominent facial features that provided irrefutable evidence that they'd shared the same womb at the same time over thirty-two years ago—the exact same rugged angle of their jaws, the strong line of their noses, and the shape of their mouths. It was like looking into a mirror and seeing a reflection of himself.

Clay blinked and shook his head, his expression dumbfounded. "What the hell . . ." Confusion deepened his voice as his words trailed off.

Tara bit her bottom lip, her gaze shifting from Clay to Jackson and back again to her boss, who was still staring at him in stunned silence, as if his brain was trying to catch up to what his eyes were actually seeing.

"Clay, this is Jackson Stone," Tara said, breaking the strained silence that had descended between them. "Your twin brother."

"My twin *brother*?" Clay exclaimed incredulously as he looked him up and down, taking in his expensive suit and no doubt judging Jackson before even knowing him. "Jesus Christ, how is that even possible . . ."

"No *fucking* way." The sibling with the sleeves of tattoos on both arms—Mason, he guessed—stared at Jackson as if he were a sideshow freak.

The brother with the lighter blond hair—clearly the cop—remained quiet, but he was no less aware as he observed Jackson through those shrewd, light green eyes of his.

Taking advantage of Clay's shock, Jackson stepped forward and extended his hand toward the other man. Hesitantly, Clay shook it, but Jackson didn't miss the immediate wariness darkening his gaze, just as Tara had warned him would happen.

"It's good to meet you. All three of you," he said, looking at each of the brothers flanking Clay as he released his twin's hand.

"We don't have a brother, so who the fuck are you, really?" the tattooed one said, his posture defensive and guarded. "Is this some kind of sick joke?"

Jackson was tempted to laugh at the absurd question, but knowing that Mason was grasping at an explanation for what he was seeing, he didn't so much as crack a smile. "No. I promise, this isn't a joke."

"Jesus, Clay," Mason said, scrubbing his fingers

through his dark hair, his disbelief still evident. "He looks *exactly* like you."

"That's because I've got a goddamn fucking *twin*," Clay replied, his raspy voice rising in volume as the reality of the situation finally started to sink in.

"How about we take this somewhere quiet and more private?" the other brother, Levi, suggested in a rational tone.

"That would be great. Thank you." Relief flooded through Jackson. At least they weren't kicking him out of the place or refusing to hear what he had to say. Hell, they could still decide that they didn't want to have anything to do with him, but once they learned the truth about the past, he hoped they could at least form some kind of relationship.

At the moment, though, these three men seemed anything but welcoming. Not that he could blame them for being cautious.

As his brothers turned around and motioned for him to follow, Jackson cast a quick glance at Tara, who'd witnessed the whole exchange. He didn't miss the worry creasing her brows, and he smiled to put her concern at ease.

"Good luck," she whispered to him.

Her support warmed him. At least he had one person on his side.

"Thank you." He mouthed the words back to her. He had a strong feeling, with these three close-knit brothers, he was going to need all the positive reinforcement he could get.

Chapter Two

A S SOON AS the four of them entered a small office in the back area of the bar, Clay closed the door for privacy and waved a hand at one of the two chairs in the room.

"Make yourself comfortable." Clay's tone was business-like as he rounded an old, scarred wooden desk and settled himself into a worn leather chair.

Lowering himself to one of the armchairs, Jackson made himself as comfortable as possible considering he felt as though he were facing a firing squad. Levi sat to his right in the other vacant seat, while Mason had brought in a wooden chair from the bar to sit in. He turned it around, straddled the seat, and rested his arms across the top, a frown on his face.

There was nothing fancy about the cramped, windowless room they were in, not compared to Jackson's luxurious private office in downtown Chicago, complete with a million-dollar view of Lake Michigan.

Everything about these three men spoke of hard-working, blue-collar roots, and he suddenly felt very out of place in his tailored suit, designer tie, and shiny Ferragamo loafers.

Shit. Maybe he should have changed from his work clothes into something more casual before coming to the bar. Too late now, and judging by the way Mason was eyeing him up and down through his narrowed gaze, the other guy had already sized him up and come to his own conclusions about Jackson.

"What proof do you have that you're our brother?" Mason asked abruptly, confirming that despite Jackson's identical looks to Clay, this other sibling wasn't going to make anything easy on him. "And what the fuck do you want with us?"

"Jesus Christ, Mason," Clay barked out in a sharp, reprimanding tone. "Cool it with the interrogation, will you? You're *looking* at irrefutable proof that he's my twin."

Mason glared at his brother, then turned that hard stare back to Jackson that was steeped with distrust and suspicion. "I want to know why he's here and what he wants."

"I don't want anything from any of you," Jackson said, his own voice brusque. "I'm here because I thought maybe you'd like to know that you had another brother."

Levi sighed, as if they were used to dealing with Mason's hotheaded behavior. "Look, I know we *all* have a lot of questions, and I'm sure Jackson will answer them, but how about we have this discussion in a civilized manner?" he said, deliberately directing the words toward his testy sibling.

"Then by all means, Mr. Calm and Rational Cop," Mason said, sarcasm lacing his voice, "since you're the expert, why don't *you* lead the interview?"

Oh, yeah, definitely a smartass.

Levi smirked and gave a *whatever* kind of shrug before glancing back at Jackson. "How long have you known about us?" he asked, his question much more logical, and far less confrontational, than his brother's.

"Not long. It's only been a couple weeks since I found out I was illegally adopted and where I came from."

"*Illegally* adopted?" Clay echoed his words as he sat up straighter in his chair, his dark brows pulled into a confused frown. "How?"

Jackson definitely had everyone's attention. Three pairs of eyes were trained on him, waiting to hear the details. "My Aunt Becca, on my mother's side of the family and who I'm very close to, told me about the adoption. My mother passed away from breast cancer when I was ten, and she made my aunt promise to never tell me the truth, but Becca felt I had the right to know about my past."

He didn't need to explain why it had taken his aunt so long to tell him the truth or how guilt had eaten away at her until she couldn't keep it a secret any longer. None of those details mattered right now, and they were personal and private to him, anyway.

He glanced across the desk to Clay, the brother he'd never known, and met his gaze. "Two weeks after I was born, our birth mother sold me to Leila, the woman who raised me as my mom, for three grand."

Clay's jaw dropped open. "She fucking *sold* you?" he asked incredulously. "For three fucking grand? Jesus Christ."

"Probably for drug money," Levi said quietly, but there was no concealing the bitterness in his tone. "I can't say I'm all that surprised."

Mason nodded in agreement, his lips stretched into a grim line. It was the only emotion he showed to indicate that their mother's heartless actions actually affected him in any way. "If you don't already know, our mother—and I use the term very lightly—was a crack whore in every sense of the word."

Jackson nodded. His aunt had told him as much, not that it made him feel any better. He should have been grateful that he'd been spared a junkie as a mother, yet there was no denying that he resented the fact that he'd never known his real brothers, one of whom was his twin. Instead, he had a sibling who was just as much of an asshole as the man who'd unwillingly raised Jackson and a father figure who'd never wanted him to begin with and made sure Jackson didn't go a day without making sure he *knew* he wasn't wanted.

"What about a birth certificate?" Clay asked, clearly trying to make sense of it all.

"My mother had one forged that I've used all my

life, but my aunt gave me my original and legal birth certificate when she told me everything a few weeks ago." Withdrawing the document he'd brought with him, Jackson unfolded the piece of paper and handed it to Mason first. "Here's the proof that you wanted to see."

The other man didn't bother to look ashamed or apologetic. Instead, Mason gave Jackson a cocky smirk before glancing at the birth certificate to verify the information before passing it on to Clay.

"How did your mother get away with an illegal adoption?" Clay asked once he'd gotten the chance to look over the official record of his birth. "Didn't anyone question the fact that she brought a baby home out of the blue?"

"My aunt said my mother told everyone that I'd been adopted through the system, and nobody questioned her. It was completely believable, so why would they doubt her claim? Soon after, my parents moved to a new city, and my so-called adoption was never brought up again and remained a secret until a couple weeks ago."

Jackson's gut churned when he remembered his conversation with his Aunt Becca and how she'd told him that Paul Stone hadn't known about his wife's unethical plan to buy a baby on the black market until Leila had brought Jackson home. By then, Paul felt trapped and as though he'd had no choice but to go along with the ruse or have his wife arrested for kidnapping or worse.

"There's no way of ever knowing how our real mother got away with selling her newborn without being caught or what lies she concocted to cover up her corrupt actions," Levi said, his voice as hard as his expression. "She's dead."

Jackson hadn't asked the PI for anything more than the information he'd received on his brothers, and even though he'd never met his birth mother, the news of her death, delivered so callously, was a shock to his system. "I'm sorry," he said automatically.

"We're not," Mason replied bluntly. "Did you miss the part where I said our mother was a crack whore? If she wasn't out getting high, she was fucking some random stranger for drug money while her kids were alone and starving at home or being abused by some prick she'd left to take care of us." Those criticizing eyes raked over Jackson once again. "Be grateful that you didn't have a shitty childhood like we did."

Jackson bit his tongue to keep from snapping back a reply. These men didn't know him or what he'd lived through. Mason was judging him based on his outer appearance alone, which irritated the hell out of Jackson because the suit he was wearing told them nothing about the man he was or what his own childhood had been like. True, he hadn't been subject-ed to a drug-addicted mother or physical abuse, but the mental and emotional torment his father had inflicted had been equally fucked up.

The room grew quiet, uncomfortably so. When none of the brothers asked any other questions,

Jackson took that as his cue that they were done.

"I know this is a lot for you guys to digest, while I've had time to process everything, so I'm going to go for now." Nobody stopped him when he stood, so he withdrew a business card from his wallet and set it on Clay's desk. "Here's my contact information. Feel free to call me if you have any other questions." *Or if you just want to get to know your long-lost brother better,* he thought, but kept the latter part to himself.

Again, no one said a word, and it left him with an empty feeling deep inside, as though he was an outsider looking in, once again, like a stranger who didn't belong. It was an emotion he hated but was all too familiar with.

He inclined his head to Clay, then the other two men. "It was good to meet all three of you," he said, then walked out of the office.

The ball was now in their court, and the next move was up to one of them.

TARA KEPT ONE eye on the hallway leading to Clay's office while filling drink orders for the few customers who'd come into the bar. She was dying to know what was going on behind that closed door. How Clay, Mason, and Levi were reacting to the news of a brother they hadn't known existed, and she was curious to find out how things were going for Jackson, too.

When it came to the Kincaid brothers, three

against one weren't great odds, especially when they perceived something, or someone, as a threat. And they'd been through enough in their lifetime to justify their wariness, even toward a man who looked identical to Clay and left no doubt in anyone's mind that they were twins.

Grabbing a bottle of rum, she poured two shots into a tall glass and filled the rest with cola, then added a lime before setting it on the serving pad for Amanda to pick up and deliver to a table. Tara had only met Jackson less than an hour ago and had talked to him for a mere thirty minutes, but she sensed he had good intentions as far as the brothers were concerned. It remained to be seen if those three men would give him any kind of chance or decide that he was someone they could trust. For Jackson's sake, she hoped the Kincaid brothers came around. She'd sensed that he wanted more than just to let them know about their long-lost brother. It was as if Jackson needed them in his life.

Fifteen short minutes after disappearing into the back room, Jackson returned by himself. Her gaze met his as he headed straight toward where she was standing behind the bar, but she couldn't get a read on his emotions. He looked like a man who knew all about control, including keeping any adverse reaction to himself.

As he neared, her traitorous body was quick to acknowledge him as a man, as it had when he'd sat at the bar earlier. A gorgeous, sexy, captivating man with a seductive mouth made for sinning and a lean, powerful body defined by the cut of his expensive suit. Even the way he walked was both sensual and assertive—and a very naughty part of her wondered if he was equally demanding in the bedroom with a woman's pleasure.

The thought alone had her panties feeling damp.

She shifted on her feet as awareness fluttered in her belly, and her heart even raced a bit faster, too. It seemed like it had been forever since she'd felt this level of temptation, this irrepressible attraction, and that was saying something considering all the men who came into the bar and hit on her on a nightly basis. She'd gone out with a few, but none of them had gotten past a date or two. And none had ever sparked the kind of burning desire she was feeling right now, without being physically touched at all.

Her response to Jackson should have felt weird, considering he was Clay's twin and she'd once had a tiny crush on her boss before he'd met and married Samantha. But while the two brothers were similar in looks, she already knew that their personalities were vastly different. This man who'd just stopped in front of her with only the counter separating them was dynamic and sophisticated, more worldly and enigmatic compared to Clay's more casual persona and the simple way he chose to live.

And he was way out of Tara's league. She considered herself an ordinary, average woman who poured drinks and managed a bar in a low- to middle-class neighborhood. And she carried around way too much baggage of guilt and regrets that sometimes felt like a hundred-pound weight on her conscience. Undoubtedly, Jackson was used to beautiful, exquisite females who were elegant and refined. Women who came from respectable families and didn't have a past crammed full of shameful secrets. There was nothing about Tara or her life that was remotely close to being cultured in any way, and there never would be.

He cocked his head to the side, his blue eyes flicking across her face before meeting her gaze again. "Warm in here?" he asked.

His odd question caught her off guard. It was the last thing she'd expected him to say after leaving Clay's office. "Umm, no. Why?"

A hint of a teasing smile tipped the corner of his mouth. "Your skin, mostly your cheeks, looks a little flushed."

Because she'd just been thinking about his prowess in the bedroom before her thoughts had veered off course. Suddenly feeling as though he'd read her mind somehow, that he knew exactly the kind of effect he had on her senses, she resisted the impulse to raise her palms to her *flushed* face.

She asked a more important question of her own instead. "How did it go in there?"

"As well as can be expected, I suppose." He shrugged nonchalantly, though she didn't miss the quick flash of disappointment that passed through his eyes before he replaced it with a wry grin. "They're a tough crowd. Mason especially."

She'd known that the brothers would be wary, standoffish, even. And she couldn't blame them considering they'd had no opportunity to process the fact that they had another sibling. "Just give them time, and I'm sure they'll come around."

He looked doubtful but didn't comment as he withdrew his wallet, pulled out a twenty, and pushed it across the counter toward her.

She eyed the money in confusion. "What's this for?"

"It's for the Bushmills I had earlier."

She quickly shook her head. "You don't have to pay for your drink—"

"Yes, I do," he countered adamantly. "I'm a paying customer just like anyone else in here. The last thing I want is to have my own brothers press charges against me for running out on my tab."

He said the words with a light amount of humor, but the underlying message in his comment made her chest tighten . . . Jackson knew the three men back in the office didn't trust him, nor had they welcomed him as family. He was still a stranger, and yeah, a paying customer.

Reluctantly, she picked up the cash, hating that she felt so torn between feeling compassion toward a man she'd just met and remaining loyal to the three brothers who were the closest thing she had to a family. She truly understood both sides of this situation and wished that the meeting had gone better for Jackson.

"Let me get your change," she said softly.

"No need," he replied before she could move toward the register. "Thanks for the conversation earlier. I enjoyed it." His voice vibrated with sincerity, and he gave her a playful wink.

She smiled at him as a sensual warmth slid through her. "I hope I see you again." And her reasons for that were partly selfish and had everything to do with him, personally, and the attraction that she had no business even thinking about, let alone acting upon.

"That all depends on those three men back in the office and whether or not they want me around." He sounded resigned to the latter. "Have a good evening, Tara."

"You, too, Jackson." She watched him go, ignoring the odd pang of disappointment inside of her in favor of ogling him one last time before he was gone. With his broad shoulders, lean hips, and confident stride, the man's backside was just as hot and mouthwatering as the rest of him.

Amanda walked up to the service area, her head turned toward Jackson's retreat, too. "Damn, he is so fine. I want to strip him naked and lick him from head to toe."

"Not if I do it first." Tara's eyes widened as she jerked her gaze to Amanda, shocked that she'd spoken her wicked thoughts out loud.

"Oh, my God, Tara," the other woman chastised with a laugh. "Did those words really just come out of your mouth?"

"Maybe," she murmured, then tried to distract the bar waitress. "What do you need?"

"I need an apple martini and a Sam's, and you obviously need to get laid." Amusement danced in Amanda's eyes. "You've never asserted a claim on any guy who's come into this bar, and you're starting with Clay's twin? I'm impressed."

That same flush of heat that Jackson had called her on less than five minutes ago suffused her cheeks once more. "I'm not claiming anyone," she insisted as she grabbed a chilled bottle of beer, popped the top, and set it on Amanda's tray before starting in on the fruity cocktail.

"It's okay. I won't tell anyone," the other woman promised in a low, conspiratorial voice. "Just remember the 'I licked it first, therefore it's mine' rule. You'd better do it before someone else does."

This time, Tara laughed. "As much as I might want to lick him, it's not going to happen."

"Why the hell not?"

"For a number of reasons." She poured the vodka and sour apple pucker into the metal shaker with bits of ice and shook the ingredients together until the alcohol was cold and slightly frothy. "For one, I have no idea if he's available, and for another, I really don't think I'm his type. Did you happen to notice that really nice suit he was wearing that probably cost a small fortune?" she asked sarcastically.

Amanda dropped a cherry into the apple martini before setting it next to the beer on her tray, then smirked at Tara. "I was too wrapped up in my own fantasy of getting him naked and licking him to notice what he was wearing. Stop getting caught up in the trivial things or you'll never have any fun."

Tara just rolled her eyes, but there was a more important detail to the equation . . . and that was the distinct possibility that she might not ever see Jackson again. There was no telling if he'd be back or not. The answer to that subject was in the hands of the three Kincaid brothers, and she suddenly wanted to know how they were dealing with the news that they had a sibling they hadn't even known about.

"Hey, Amanda," Tara said as the other woman was about to leave the counter. "After you deliver those drinks, are your tables good for a while?"

"Yep. Do you need me to cover for you so you can run to the little girls' room?"

Amanda split her time between cocktail waitressing and bartending at Kincaid's, depending on what was needed for the night. Wednesdays were the slowest evenings of the week, so Amanda took the waitress shift. "Actually, I'd like to go talk to Clay and it might be more than a few minutes."

"Sure, fine. I can handle the bar and Gina can cover the floor for a while," she said of the other bar waitress and part-time bartender who was also working for the night. "Give me a sec to take care of these drinks, and I'll be back."

A few minutes later, Tara was heading toward Clay's office. Deep, masculine voices drifted out into the hallway, and when she reached the door, it was open a few inches. She knocked lightly to announce her presence, then poked her head inside.

"You guys okay?" she asked as she slipped into the office.

"No, we're not fucking okay." Mason jammed his hands through his hair as he paced back and forth in the small space, his agitation coming through loud and clear. "We have a goddamn brother we knew nothing about, not to mention finding out our mother sold Clay's twin for fucking drug money."

She sucked in a startled breath. "Is that what Jackson told you?"

"Yeah." Mason's jaw hardened even more, and Levi and Clay remained quiet while their brother continued to rant. "I wouldn't believe it if it weren't for the fact that selling a kid is exactly something our sorry excuse for a mother would do. That bitch had no conscience."

Her head spun as Mason's words eventually sunk in, and she couldn't imagine how Jackson had felt hearing that devastating news for the first time. And she was doing it again . . . feeling empathy for a man she'd just met.

"Then he comes in here with his flashy, high-dollar suit, and oh, hey, look, he's a goddamn architect at some big fucking firm in Chicago," Mason went on cynically while flicking his finger over the glossy business card he held in his hand. "Jesus, he looks as though he grew up with a silver spoon in his mouth, while we barely scraped by every single day."

"You don't know what his childhood was like, and just because he might have money and a respectable job, it doesn't make him a bad person." She didn't bother to point out that Clay had over a million dollars tucked away, a tidy sum of money, along with the bar he'd inherited from the old man who'd owned the place before he'd passed away. And no one was judging him based on his wealth and what he'd been given.

Mason crossed his tattooed arms over his wide chest, his stance defensive. "I don't trust him." And for a man who'd had very little reason to let other people into the Kincaid inner circle, it was as simple as that.

"I'll see what I can find out about Jackson," Levi finally said, his voice even and practical. "I have someone at the station who owes me a favor, and I'll get them to run a thorough background check on the guy to see if he has anything glaring in his past. Or any kind of record or issues that we should be concerned about."

"That's kind of invasive, don't you think?" Tara asked, the comment escaping her before she realized just how biased her question sounded.

"We have no idea who he is." Clay was still sitting behind his desk, and he leaned back in his chair as his gaze met Tara's. "Not really."

"Or what he wants," Mason piped in once more.

She laughed, but the sound lacked any real humor.

"What if he just wants to get to know the three brothers that he was separated from at birth?"

Clay frowned at her. "Why are you defending him?"

The room grew quiet as three pairs of eyes studied her way too intently. "I'm not defending him."

"Yeah, you are," Mason said, his voice gruff as his suspicious gaze narrowed even further. "Did Jackson get inside your head before we got here? Is that why you're on his side?"

"*What?*" She gaped at Mason, unable to believe that he'd just accused Jackson of brainwashing her. Exasperation and frustration made her voice rise a few notches. "Oh, my God. *No*, he didn't get inside my head. He asked about you guys. He was genuinely interested in knowing about all three of you."

"And what did you tell him?" Levi asked.

"Just general stuff that he could find out on his own if he wanted to." That was the truth. She hadn't revealed anything personal or private.

Clay scrubbed a hand along his unshaven jaw and sighed heavily. "If Jackson comes around again, stay away from him until Levi finds out more about who he is."

She was used to Clay being protective, and normally she appreciated his concern, but there was nothing that Jackson had said or done during his short time in the bar that had led her to believe he was dangerous in any way. "He doesn't seem like a serial killer to me," she said.

"You don't know that," Mason said, bickering with her as if *she* were a sibling.

She gave him a barely tolerable look. "You're impossible, you know that? How does Katrina put up with you on a daily basis?" When he smirked, she held up her hand to cut him off, knowing he was about to spout off something inappropriate and crass. "Never mind. Don't answer that."

Her imploring gaze sought out Clay's instead, because out of the three brothers, she knew he was the least likely person in this room to make assumptions about a person's character based on outward appearance and one fifteen-minute conversation. She knew this because Clay had taken a chance on her when she'd had nothing and no one. When she'd been so lost and alone and needed just one person to believe in her. He'd given her that faith.

"Don't be so quick to cast judgment against Jackson before you get to know him. That's not what you do or who you are, Clay." There was a reason he'd been nicknamed Saint Clay, and she appealed to that kindness and altruistic side of his personality now. "You've always seen the good in people, and you've always given them a chance to prove themselves and their integrity. Jackson is your twin brother, and he deserves that chance."

Clay nodded in understanding but didn't soften completely. "He's a stranger, and I'm just trying to protect my family," he said quietly.

"And I respect that." She truly did, especially after

all that they'd been through. "I just don't want the three of you to have any regrets later on."

Knowing she'd said enough, she decided it was time for her to leave the office. "I need to get back to the bar," she said, and turned to go.

"Tara?"

At the sound of Clay calling her name, she faced him again, wondering if she'd said too much or had gone too far. "Yes?"

"Next Saturday, schedule yourself off for the day and night," Clay said. "Amanda can handle things for the evening."

Not what she'd expected at all. As the manager of Kincaid's—a position Clay had promoted her to when she'd finally finished her college courses a few weeks ago and could devote more time to the business side of the bar—she always worked weekends. Amanda was trained to close the bar with the help of a few other employees, but she found Clay's request an odd one.

She tipped her head curiously. "Okay. Mind if I ask why?"

A fond smile curved his lips, all traces of their more serious conversation about Jackson gone. "Because Samantha, Katrina, and Sarah decided that's when we're having a barbeque at our place to celebrate you graduating from college and getting your business degree. Did you really think we were going to let something huge like that go by without recognition?"

She swallowed back the swell of emotion that rose

in her throat, but there was nothing she could do about the warmth she could feel sweeping across her cheeks. "You don't have to do that. It's not a big deal."

"It's a huge fucking deal," Mason said affectionately. "We're proud of you. Between school and exams and being at the bar, you worked your ass off. Besides, it's a great excuse to drink, party, and get wild and crazy."

"Of course it is," she said on a laugh. "It sounds like fun. Thank you."

Leave it to the Kincaid brothers to surprise her with something so sweet. Which just made her feel a little guilty for backing Jackson and pushing for them to give him the benefit of the doubt. She told herself she'd done it for them, and she had. But she couldn't deny the part of her that wanted to see Jackson Stone again.

Chapter Three

FEELING MOODY AND restless, Jackson stood in front of the floor-to-ceiling window in the living room of his Lake Shore condo, staring out at the myriad of lights twinkling below as dusk settled over the city. It had been one hell of a long fucking week at work, from numerous client presentations to attending a ground-breaking ceremony for a new office building in downtown Chicago to handling environmental issues that had come across his desk. He'd sat through a dozen long, drawn-out meetings with engineering consultants and had stayed late most nights discussing a structural issue that was causing massive delays on one of the firm's billion-dollar projects.

Tonight, he'd actually gotten home at a reasonable hour, if a regular person considered nine in the evening normal, he thought wryly. He'd taken a long, hot shower, heated up leftover spaghetti he'd had in the refrigerator for dinner, and eaten the meal while reviewing some proposals he'd brought home with him. But here in his condo, where it was too damn quiet and there weren't any hectic demands constantly diverting his attention, his mind taunted him with the harsh knowledge that he clearly wasn't good enough to be welcomed into the Kincaid family.

Leaning against the back of the leather couch a few feet away from the plate-glass window, he rubbed at the tension settling in his neck and shoulders. Seven days had passed since he'd walked into Clay's bar and met his brothers for the first time. Seven days without any contact from them. Their silence spoke louder than words and cut deeper than a knife, and he fucking hated that their rejection affected him on any kind of emotional level. That their approval and acceptance mattered that much to him, because it was the one thing in his life that Paul Stone had cruelly and deliberately deprived him of.

Fuck. He'd never been one to feel sorry for himself. He was a man who made things happen and didn't wallow in things he couldn't change. But he'd be lying if he didn't admit that he'd foolishly believed that by reaching out to the men who shared the same genes as him, it would finally give him that sense of belonging that had eluded him his whole life. But so far, making contact with the Kincaid brothers had only brought him a wealth of disappointment and frustration.

The three of them had made it very clear, or at least Mason had, that they doubted his intentions and believed he had ulterior motives, and Jackson knew there was nothing else he could say or do to sway their opinion. The next move was up to them, and after last week's confrontation in Clay's office, he had a feeling that hell might freeze over before any of them made any kind of contact.

But Tara . . . the beautiful bartender was nothing like the terse, skeptical men he'd faced off with. Despite the vulnerable edge he'd detected in her, she'd been warm and encouraging, so sweet and easy to talk to—the total opposite of the women he normally interacted with in his social circle. Tara hadn't prejudged him based on his appearance, hadn't made assumptions about his character based on preconceived notions. Instead, she'd willingly given him what the Kincaid brothers had withheld . . . unconditional acceptance. And that open and trusting approach, along with that spark of mutual attraction between them, had visions of her drifting through his mind as he lay in bed at night trying to fall asleep.

His thoughts of Tara always started off innocently enough—remembering her sweet smile or recalling the way that diamond stud above her lip caught the light when she glanced his way—but those chaste images never lasted long before they strayed down a path rife with filthy, forbidden fantasies. The kind that had her splayed out on his bed for his pleasure, naked and needy and begging, while his mouth and fingers and cock did unspeakably dirty things to that soft, wet spot between her legs before he drove balls deep inside of her.

He momentarily closed his eyes and groaned as a jolt of lust tightened in his groin. A familiar throb took up residence, and he didn't dare press his palm over the hard column of flesh pushing against the soft cotton shorts he'd put on after his shower, because he didn't trust himself not to wrap his hand around his dick and jerk off right there in front of the windows in his living room.

Jesus, he needed a distraction. He considered turning on his laptop to review the specs he'd just received on an upcoming project, but his mind wasn't in work mode. He could call his best friend, Wes Sinclair, to meet him at The Popped Cherry, a trendy bar they frequented in downtown Chicago, but he wasn't in the mood for the kind of socializing that usually led to fending off women he had no interest in. Or he could always go to bed early, but Jackson wasn't tired, and, well, he knew how that would end . . .

He knew where he *wanted* to be. The same place he'd thought about going back to for the past week, and it had nothing to do with wanting to see his brothers again and everything to do with the sexy bartender he couldn't get out of his head.

Fuck it. He glanced back at the clock on the wall. It was nearly ten at night on a Wednesday. He knew Kincaid's closed at eleven Sunday through Thursday—yeah, he'd looked up that information because this wasn't the first time he'd contemplated a return. The strained way things had ended with his siblings had kept him from following through on the impulse, but tonight, he didn't give a shit if Clay, Mason, or Levi had an issue with him being at the bar. Kincaid's was open to the public, and he was a paying customer.

The gloom hanging over him dissipated as anticipation took its place. Before he talked himself out of his spontaneous decision, he changed into a pair of jeans and a casual shirt and arrived at Kincaid's twenty minutes after leaving his condo.

He walked inside the establishment. Rock music played through the sound system, but the place was surprisingly empty. No customers, and he didn't see the two bar waitresses from last week, either. He did hear voices and sounds coming from an area that appeared to be a kitchen, so he assumed the bar was still open, even if it was a slow night.

He glanced over at the bar, and a smile curved his lips as he caught a side view of Tara as she wiped down the counter, probably cleaning up for the night since they closed in half an hour. She was singing along to "You Give Love a Bad Name" by Bon Jovi, oblivious to the fact that he was standing just out of her line of vision. Which he didn't mind one bit, because it gave him the opportunity to watch as her breasts swayed against her tight T-shirt each time her arm swept back and forth across the surface of the bar, and she shook her perfect ass and swayed her hips in time to the beat.

Heat coursed through his veins and his cock stirred. Oh, yeah, he was feeling *much* better already.

Relaxed and amused and getting more and more aroused with every second that passed. All thoughts of work fled, along with thoughts of his brothers. Just seeing this woman seemed to calm the storm of emotions that had been raging through him earlier.

This was exactly what he needed. *She* was what he needed. Tara provided a lighthearted diversion in a life that suddenly felt much too complicated, and she also made him realize how much he'd missed *wanting* to be around a woman for the sheer pleasure and enjoyment of it. Without any pressures or expectations.

As Tara sang the ending lyrics to the song, she glanced his way and did a quick double take. Much to his disappointment, she abruptly stopped cleaning the counter, which meant her bouncing tits came to a standstill and she no longer rolled her hips in a way that made him envision her sitting astride his cock, gyrating on top of him, and giving him a provocative lap dance using the same sensual technique.

Those gorgeous blue eyes rounded in surprise at seeing him, then quickly ebbed to genuine delight. "Jackson," she said, her voice breathless, and he didn't think it was from all her singing and dancing.

"You recognized me," he teased as he came up to the other side of the bar across from where she was standing. The fact that she could tell him apart from his twin this time told Jackson that he at least had some distinctive traits.

A sexy, mischievous grin found a place on her full, kissable lips. "Of course I recognized you. Clay has never stared at my ass before, and he's never looked at me like he wants to . . ." As if she belatedly realized how much she'd been about to divulge, her words trailed off and her soft, creamy complexion turned blush pink.

Don't go all shy on me now, sweetheart. It was the last thing he wanted with her, and he dared to finish that sentence, just to test the flirtatious waters between them. "Like he wants to do bad, dirty things to you?"

Tara swallowed hard but never broke eye contact with him. "Umm, yes. That." She sounded flustered but not at all offended by his blatant words that summed up just how strongly he was attracted to her.

"Guilty as charged." His tone was playful as he slid onto one of the empty barstools across from her. "On both accounts." Because yeah, he'd stared at her perky ass and he definitely wanted to do wicked things with her.

She laughed, the sound just as inviting as she was. "At least you're honest."

"Always," he said, and meant it. After being lied to his entire life, about numerous things, integrity was the thing he valued the most, in himself and from other people.

"If you're looking for Clay, he isn't here," she said, obviously assuming the reason for his visit.

He smiled at her. "I didn't think he would be."

"Oh." She tipped her head to the side, looking adorably curious. "Then what brings you by?"

He met her gaze. Held it intently. "You."

CARLY PHILLIPS & ERIKA WILDE

She looked both shocked and undeniably pleased. "Why me?"

"I believe we just established the *why*," he said with humor as he clasped his hands on the bar. He wasn't one to play games and decided to take the direct approach so she'd have no doubts about his interest in her. "But just in case you missed all that flirtatious banter about me eyeing your sexy backside—and maybe, if I'm lucky, eventually we'll do dirty, bad things together—I'm very attracted to you. I *thought* the attraction was reciprocated."

"It was. It *is*," she added, quick to change past tense to present. "I just thought you were here to see one of the guys."

He shook his head. "Unfortunately, they have no desire to see me." Saying the words out loud felt like a physical punch to the gut. "I haven't heard from any of them since last week, so I'm pretty sure I'm persona non grata around here. But I thought you were worth the risk of getting thrown out on my ass if one of them happened to be here."

She didn't laugh at his comment as he'd hoped. Instead, her lips flattened into a disappointed frown. "I'm sorry that the guys are being so stubborn and shortsighted about you."

"Don't be." He shrugged it off, not wanting to get into a conversation about his brothers' rejection. "It is what it is." With every day that passed, he was becoming more resigned to the possibility that the situation might not ever change.

"Yeah, good mantra," she said, her eyes suddenly sparkling with approval. "It's mine, too. It's gotten me through some tough times in life."

He wanted to know about those difficult circumstances. Wanted to know why there was a slight edge to her yet she could be so kind and compassionate, too. It was a combination he found intriguing and tempting, and it made him want to peel back all those fascinating layers to discover all of the secrets that lay beneath.

"Would you like something to drink?" she asked, pulling his attention back to her. "Bushmills, neat?"

"Not tonight." It was late, and he didn't want any alcohol to dull his senses, not when he was around her. "I'll have a soda water with lime."

While she made his drink, he withdrew his wallet, pulled out a ten-dollar bill, and pushed it across the counter toward her as she set his order on a cocktail napkin in front of him.

"Keep the change," he said.

"Seriously?" She crossed her arms over her chest in annoyance and eyed the money but didn't pick it up. "It's soda water, for heaven's sake."

"I know exactly what it is," he said, squeezing the lime into the sparkling water before dropping the piece of fruit into the liquid. "But that's not the point."

He'd already made that particular *point* last week when he'd paid for his drink then, as well. It was an argument she wasn't going to win.

She knew it, too, because she picked up the cash

with a frustrated sigh. "I see you have your brothers' obstinate streak."

"Must be a family trait." He bit the inside of his cheek, trying not to laugh at how cute she looked being miffed with him. Cute *and* hot, he amended as his gaze focused on those pouty lips of hers . . . which then transitioned to lustful thoughts of her soft mouth and all the ways he'd imagined defiling it.

She turned away to put the money into the cash register, and predictably, his eyes lowered to her perfectly rounded ass. Jesus, he was such a fucking pervert. Not wanting to get caught leering at her again, he made sure he was looking above her chest by the time she faced him again.

"What time do you get out of here tonight?" he asked, then took a drink of his lime-flavored water.

She began washing glasses in a small sink behind the bar. "I'm the only one in the bar closing up. It was so slow I sent the waitresses home. The guys in the kitchen finish with their clean-up around eleven thirty, so that's when I lock up."

"Any plans after that?"

"At midnight?" She laughed as she dried a martini glass. "The only plan I have is to crawl into my nice, soft bed with a book and read until I fall asleep."

And there went his rampant thoughts again as he envisioned her in his bed, stripped naked and legs spread, her creamy skin a stark contrast to his navy blue comforter and all that thick, luxurious black hair spread across his white pillow. No doubt, if he had her anywhere near his bed, reading or sleeping would be the last thing she'd be doing.

Not that they were going to have sex tonight, but it wasn't as though he hadn't thought of the possibility of fucking her. Yeah, that was a nightly fantasy that always left him hard and aching. Just like he was beginning to feel now.

He shifted on the barstool in lieu of reaching down to adjust his dick that was pressing against the fly of his jeans. Grateful that she didn't have a view of his lap and his lack of physical restraint when it came to thoughts of getting down and dirty with her, he shifted the conversation back on track.

"I know I might be cutting into your beauty sleep, but would you like to go and get a coffee at that twenty-four-hour donut shop down the road once you're off for the night?"

Any other woman he'd gone out with in the past would have scoffed at the suggestion of going to what they'd consider a substandard eatery, let alone accompany him to this run-down neighborhood in Chicago. But Tara's eyes lit up at the invitation.

She batted her eyes at him in a playful manner. "Are you asking me out on a date, Mr. Stone?"

"Yes." A part of him was relieved she hadn't flat out turned him down. She at least looked as though she was considering his offer. "I'd take you somewhere far more impressive, but there's not much open at this time of the night."

"Lucky for you, donuts are my weakness and one

of the few things I can't resist," she said, rearranging a few of the bottles of alcohol that were lined up in a bin. "And oh, my God, Angelo makes *the* best apple fritters in the entire city, and just thinking about them is making my mouth water."

Her enthusiasm made him grin. "Is that a yes?"

"That is a *hell* yeah," she said, and laughed.

Now that he'd secured more time with Tara, he let her continue with her clean-up of the bar, doing his best not to distract her so she'd finish as soon as possible. At eleven straight up, she locked the main doors and cashed out the register and took the money back to the office. While she was gone, a young kid came out from the back area and began putting chairs up on the tables.

As he swept the floor, he kept one eye on Jackson, and it was clear that the kid had heard about him and couldn't decide if he was a threat of some sort or not. It all depended on what information had filtered through the gossip mill about his meeting with the Kincaid brothers. If Mason was to be believed, then Jackson was sure he was branded as public enemy number one.

"That's Elijah," Tara said when she came back from whatever she was doing in the office and saw him glancing at the boy. "He's a great kid. Clay found him rummaging through the dumpster for something to eat and gave him a job."

Before Jackson could reply, a man's voice spoke.

"Tara, are you about finished up?" the guy asked as

he limped into the bar area. "The kitchen is clean and—"

His words abruptly stopped as the man's one good eye that wasn't covered with a patch stared at Jackson in that way he was becoming all too familiar with. Perceptive and a whole lot standoffish. Now that the employees at Kincaid's knew about him, they weren't so quick to assume he was Clay.

"You must be the twin," the other man said gruffly.

"That would be me," he replied in a pleasant tone as he extended his hand toward the man in a friendly gesture since he was standing close enough. "I'm Jackson."

The guy hesitated, then finally stepped forward and clasped Jackson's hand in his strong, unrelenting grip, silently sending a message Jackson would have had to be an idiot to miss. This man was clearly Team Kincaid, and if handshakes could talk, this one would say *you do anything even remotely sketchy and I will gladly kick your ass.*

"Hank," he said brusquely, introducing himself before he glanced at Tara behind the bar. "You almost done out here?"

"Yes." She stacked a few racks of clean glasses on top of each other. "If you and Elijah are finished, you can go ahead and leave. I'll have Jackson walk me out to my car."

A muscle in Hank's jaw ticked. "I don't think Clay would be too happy if he found out—"

Tara held up a hand. "Let me deal with Clay, okay? The boys might have a personal issue with Jackson, but I don't. Since they aren't here and I'm in charge, I'm assuring you that I'll be absolutely fine in this man's company, so I'll see you and Elijah tomorrow afternoon for your shifts."

Boom. Mic drop.

Jackson tamped down the grin threatening to appear. Beautiful *and* defiant—a woman who knew her own mind and was strong enough to assert herself when warranted. Another huge fucking turn-on, especially when he thought about controlling that rebellious streak of hers in the bedroom. Calling the shots. Pinning her down while she bucked beneath the onslaught of his mouth and fingers. Taking her hard and deep and demanding her surrender.

He exhaled a slow breath, which helped, somewhat, to banish those images from his mind. Hank scowled at him one more time—*and thank fucking God he wasn't a mind reader*—but didn't argue further with Tara. Within the next five minutes, Elijah and Hank were both gone, leaving him alone with Tara.

"You all are a loyal bunch, aren't you?" he asked wryly.

"Hank's a good guy," she said as she bent down to retrieve her purse from a locked cupboard. "But yeah, he's loyal, too. He's former military and he lost his leg and right eye to an IED, which also caused facial nerve damage. Clay hired Hank when no one else would."

Jesus, there was no way he could compete with

Saint Clay. Not on any level. As much as his twin irked him for being so cool and reserved with Jackson, he had a lot of respect for the man and how he treated people. It said a lot about Clay's character and the kind man he was. One with integrity, despite his shitty upbringing.

"Is this donut date going to be an issue with the guys?" he asked, keeping his question light and humorous as he slid off his barstool. Jackson didn't want to give a fuck what any of his brothers thought about his interest in Tara, but he also didn't want them to give her flack about him, either.

She came around the bar, keys in hand as she switched off the lights in the main area. "As much as I love those three guys like they're my brothers, they don't have a say in who I see." Now that she was on the same side of the bar as him, she stopped an arm's length away and met his gaze. "Are you having second thoughts about me?"

The unexpected hint of doubt and insecurity swimming in her blue eyes had him instinctively reaching out to touch her, to reassure her that he wasn't a man easily intimidated when he wanted something. And his desire for Tara was only growing stronger, not lessening in any way, and he wasn't ready to walk away from whatever was happening between them.

He brushed his fingers along the soft skin of her jaw, and when her lips parted slightly and her eyes softened, it took every ounce of restraint he had not to slide his hand around the back of her neck and pull her mouth up to his for a hot, deep, claiming kiss. Instead, he settled with the knowledge that she wouldn't have stopped him if he had followed through with the impulse. Her clear consent would have to be enough for now, because he didn't think he'd be able to stop with just one taste.

He gently caressed his thumb along her full bottom lip before dropping his hand back down to his side. "Believe me when I say I'm not even close to changing my mind about you," he promised her.

Her tongue skimmed across the place his finger had just touched, and she looked up at him with a smile that was filled with relief and quickly turned to bright-eyed sass. "Good. Now let's go get donuts."

Chapter Four

JACKSON GLANCED IN his rearview mirror to make sure Tara was still following his car. The donut shop was only a few blocks away, but she'd insisted on driving herself, which was fine with him. But considering the area, he wanted to keep a close eye on her and her vehicle until they arrived and he had her safely inside the place.

Which was ridiculous, considering Tara seemed street smart and perfectly capable of taking care of herself. She gave him the distinct impression that she could handle all sorts of trouble without the help of a man, but he was quickly discovering that she roused protective instincts in him that he was finding hard to shake. In a short time, she'd gotten under his skin, and it was even more shocking that he'd allowed his fascination with her to evolve into something close to an obsession. And now here he was, taking Tara on a date, of all things, when it was nearly midnight on a work night.

He grinned and shook his head at the insane situation. He was going to be exhausted tomorrow at the office, but he didn't really care. For the first time since his divorce three years ago, he actually wanted to get to know a woman better, instead of bypassing any kind of getting-to-know-you conversation and getting down to the basics of sex and physical release.

His infatuation with Tara was out of character for him, but he wasn't going to question such a strong, instantaneous connection to this woman when so much in his life had been clouded with uncertainty and that vague sense that something was missing. With the discovery of his adoption and having a twin brother, he now understood where that void stemmed from and why he'd always struggled with a disconnect from his own family.

There was something about Tara and her lack of judgment about who he was that made him feel as though he finally fit in somewhere, that maybe, possibly, he'd found someone who truly understood him.

The illuminated sign for Angelo's Donuts came into view, and Jackson turned into the small corner lot and parked his car behind the brick building. Tara's older-model Toyota took the space next to his Porsche, and they both got out of their vehicles at the same time and met up behind his.

"Nice ride," she said, nodding her head toward his shiny gray Carrera. "Aren't you afraid your car might get jacked in this neighborhood?"

The thought had crossed his mind, but he wasn't about to admit it and come off as an egotistical jerk who had an issue being in her part of the city. "That's what LoJack and insurance are for, right?" he said of the tracking and recovery system he'd purchased with the car.

She laughed lightly. "I guess so. Hopefully you won't have to put it to the test."

They walked toward the front of the building, where two police cars were parked. The uniformed officers were standing by the trunks of one of their vehicles, drinking coffee and eating a donut while shooting the shit with each other. He glanced at the men, expecting one of them to be Levi—because of course that would be just his luck—but neither of their faces was familiar.

Jackson placed a hand on the small of Tara's back as an excuse to touch her as he guided her toward the front entrance, nodding toward the show of law enforcement. "I don't think I have to worry too much about my car," he said in a low voice. "The place looks pretty well protected."

"Yeah, the cops around here love Angelo's." As they passed the officers, Tara gave them a friendly nod, then said in a low voice only Jackson could hear, "Then again, what decent cop doesn't like a good donut?"

He chuckled as he opened the glass door for her. "That's so cliché."

"I know, but it made you laugh."

She gave him a cheeky grin as she brushed past him with a bounce in her step, and he had to resist the urge to smack her ass for being so impudent. The fact that he was that comfortable with her, this quickly, should have had him throwing up his walls to keep his emotional distance, but instead he let himself embrace the relaxed, easygoing sensation coursing through him. Tonight was all about enjoying himself with Tara, without second-guessing or over-examining whatever this was developing between them.

Surprisingly, for as late as it was, there were a few people in the shop, testimony to just how good the treats in this place were. As they walked up to the glass display housing an array of different donuts, a young man who looked to be in his early twenties grinned at Tara.

"Hey, Tara, it's good to see you," the dark-haired man with a slight Italian accent said. His gaze shifted to Jackson, the same friendly smile on his face. "And what are you doing here so late? Don't you have a wife at home waiting for you? Or are you here because she's got a late-night craving?"

"Dante, this isn't Clay," Tara explained quickly, because clearly the guy was referring to Clay's wife, Samantha. "It's his twin brother, Jackson. And this is Dante, Angelo's son," she said.

Dante's brows shot up to his forehead. "Oh, wow . . . "

Jackson braced himself for that adverse reaction he

was getting used to, like the one he'd just been dealt back at the bar with Hank. But Dante clearly didn't know the dynamics of the situation that made Jackson an outsider to the Kincaid clan, because he didn't hesitate to thrust his hand across the counter for Jackson to shake.

"Nice to meet you, man," Dante said without an ounce of awkwardness between them, his tone completely sincere. "What can I get for you two?"

"I'll take a large black coffee and an apple fritter," Jackson said, going with Tara's recommendation.

Tara bit her bottom lip, an indecisive frown creasing her brows as she looked into the display case. "Now that I'm here, I can't decide. Do I want the donut with the sprinkles on it, the chocolate French cruller, or the apple fritter?"

"How about all three?" Jackson suggested.

She gave him a sexy sidelong glance. "Are you trying to seduce me with donuts?"

"I might be." He winked at her.

A small, beguiling smile curved up the corner of her mouth. She certainly didn't appear opposed to the idea, and he had to shove his hands into the front pockets of his jeans so he didn't drag her out of here and make good on that promise.

Tara glanced back at Dante. "I'll have a coffee and an apple fritter, too," she told him.

The kid bagged their donuts and set their items on the counter. Jackson paid for their order, and while Tara stopped to put cream and sugar into her coffee, he carried their late-night snack to a vacant table away from the front area so they'd have some privacy. She joined him a few minutes later and took a seat across from him.

Once they each had one of the deep-fried donuts set out on a napkin in front of them—still warm from being freshly made—he watched as she pulled off a corner and popped it into her mouth. She chewed and a soft moan rumbled up from her throat as she closed her eyes as if to savor the taste. But all Jackson could think about was her making that same arousing sigh of pleasure while he was buried deep inside her body. Another bite, and she made the same sound again, and this time his cock hardened with lust.

Fuck. "Please don't do that." His voice sounded strangled. *He* felt strangled.

Her guileless gaze met his, and she looked genuinely confused. "Do what?"

He swallowed his own bite of fritter, and damn, it *was* that good. "Moan like that."

It took her a moment to catch his understanding, but when she did, the wicked light that glimmered in her gorgeous blue eyes tempted and enticed him, as did the sparkle of the diamond above her lip. "Like what?" she dared.

Did she really think he wouldn't accept that challenge? He leaned across the table, his voice low and direct. "Like you're in the throes of an orgasm."

"I can't help myself." Her perfectly straight teeth grazed her bottom lip, scraping off a smudge of sugary glaze that he wanted to lick off for himself. "These fritters are crispy and buttery and sweet and all the bad things I shouldn't have."

He took a sip of his coffee, his eyes meeting hers from over the rim of the paper cup for a moment before he set it back down. "Am I one of those bad things?" he teased.

"Probably." An emotion he couldn't name crossed her features, bringing with it a vulnerability that changed the undertone of their flirty exchange and made her expression turn more serious than he'd intended. "But there's something about you I find hard to say no to."

He felt the same compelling attraction. "Then don't," he said, meaning it.

A wry smile tipped up the corner of her mouth. "There's so many reasons I *should* say no."

"Clay, Mason, and Levi?" he guessed.

She shook her head as she ate another bite of her donut, much more demurely this time and without the sound effects that had led them down this path of conversation in the first place. "Believe it or not, they aren't at the top of the list."

Surprise flickered through him. "Care to tell me what is?"

She wrapped her slender fingers around her paper cup, seemingly considering his question, but something ultimately held her back from confiding in him. "No. I'd rather not."

"Fair enough." Was he disappointed not to discover why she believed she shouldn't be here with him? Absolutely, but he wasn't one to push or pry, and what he wanted more than anything was to get them back to that place where they were both comfortable with one another. "Then how about you tell me how long you've been working for Clay?"

She latched onto the safer topic and smiled. "It's been about six years. I started at Kincaid's as a cocktail waitress, and he eventually trained me as a bartender while I went to school part-time for a business degree."

Jackson recalled their conversation from last week, when she'd told him that she'd been one of those employees Clay had hired because she'd been down on her luck. More questions rose to the surface, but he decided to let her reveal what she wanted, in her own time. Now that they'd established more than just a casual acquaintance, he didn't want to give her an opportunity to pull away, which would be too easy for her to do since she'd just expressed doubts about him.

"Now that I've finally graduated and have my business degree, Clay promoted me to manager of Kincaid's," she went on, picking another piece of fried dough off her fritter. "With me in charge and handling the main operation of the bar, it allows him to be home with Samantha a lot more, especially now that she's pregnant."

An unexpected pang of envy struck Jackson, and he resisted the urge to rub at the slice of pain in his chest. "He's a lucky man." It seemed his brother had the kind of perfect life Jackson himself once believed he'd had, as well. Getting married, having a devoted wife, envisioning a future with a family of his own. Yeah, Jackson had once thought he'd had everything he'd wanted since he was a young boy—unconditional love, a sense of security, and someone to create a solid life with—until he'd been blindsided by yet another betrayal by the one person he should have been able to trust the most. Unfortunately, his wife had been more interested in fucking one of his colleagues than being faithful to him and had ultimately chosen that same guy to marry once the ink was barely dry on their divorce papers. She'd gone on to have a kid with him, further twisting that knife she'd stabbed into Jackson's heart, since he'd thought *they'd* been trying to conceive at the time.

Collette was yet another person who'd not only deceived him but made him feel as though he wasn't good enough. Was it any wonder he had issues when it came to trusting people with his emotional well-being? His entire life had been a farce and filled with rejection, and his marriage had been a complete sham. His track record sucked.

He pushed thoughts of his ex-wife from his mind, far more interested in Tara's story. "Now that you have a degree, are you going to find another job, in a different field?"

"No." She hesitated, fiddling with the corner of her napkin, then seemingly decided to explain why. "I wanted a degree because . . . well, it helped me focus on something positive at a time in my life when I desperately needed a direction. I'm perfectly content where I am, and Clay is incredibly generous when it comes to my salary. Not only do I enjoy working at Kincaid's, a part of me owes Clay for . . ." She shook her head and glanced away. "Never mind. It doesn't matter."

She pretended interest in drinking her coffee, and he was beginning to realize that this woman was full of deep, difficult secrets. He wanted to know what she'd been about to say, because the pain he'd momentarily glimpsed in her eyes *did* matter to him. But again, he traded in one topic for another.

"Does your family live around here?" he asked, hoping that was an easier subject for her to talk about.

Another strained smile told him he'd missed the mark. "No. My father is an army sergeant at Camp Butler in Springfield, which is about two hundred miles away from here. My parents have lived there for about ten years now and I don't see them much. My brother is also career military and is currently stationed in Germany."

He tipped his head, curious to know why she'd live so far away from her family. "So what brought you to Chicago?"

"I needed a change." She shrugged, her reply just as vague as the rest of their exchange. "What about you? What is your family like?"

Now that *he* was in the hot seat, he understood Tara's reluctance to delve into parts of her life that were less than perfect or ideal. He finished his coffee, debating where to best start to describe the people who'd raised him.

"I'll admit I'm curious to hear how you were adopted," she went on when he remained quiet for too long, more relaxed now that she wasn't the focus of their discussion. "Clay said his mother sold you to the woman who raised you for three grand . . ." Her voice trailed off, a sudden apologetic look passing across her expression. "I'm sorry. If you'd rather not talk about it, I completely understand."

"No, it's okay," he assured her.

Since learning the truth from his aunt, the only three people he'd told about the illegal adoption were Clay, Mason, and Levi. Up until this point, he'd kept everything to himself because the situation was so fucked up, and honestly, he was still trying to come to terms with his true identity—as a Kincaid and not a Stone as he'd believed his entire life.

"It's true," he confirmed of his birth mother's actions, and told the story as he'd heard it from his Aunt Becca a few weeks ago. "My mother, Leila, didn't think she could have kids. My father and she tried for years, and when she couldn't get pregnant, they went to a specialist who confirmed she had endometriosis, and even though she underwent surgery, the doctor told her that, without fertility treatments, the likelihood of her conceiving were slim to none. At the time, my father was just getting his construction business started, and they couldn't afford the cost of in vitro fertilization, but my mother was desperate for a baby."

Tara sat back in her chair, her eyes soft and compassionate as she listened intently. He had to admit that it felt good to really talk about what had happened with someone who was sincerely interested in hearing the details, unlike his brothers, who'd only heard the bare facts and had barely believed those as it was.

He exhaled and continued on. "Someone at the diner where my mother worked told her they knew a way she could get a newborn. They set her up with a guy who was a go-between for my birth mom, who was a junkie looking to sell one of her twins for money to buy more drugs. Three thousand dollars in cash later, my mother had the baby she thought she'd never have."

"She must have wanted you very badly to go to such extremes."

"I'm sure she did," he agreed, though he couldn't stop the bitterness that rose to the surface. "My father, though? Not so much. From the moment Leila brought me home and he found out she'd bought me from a crack whore and prostitute, he didn't want to have anything to do with me. But he also realized that they were stuck with a baby she'd essentially bought on the black market, along with the lies my mother told people about how they'd adopted me through *legal* channels. I felt his resentment every day of my life."

He hadn't realized he'd clenched his fist on the table until she reached a hand across the space separating them and placed her cool fingers on his tense arm.

He looked into her deep blue eyes, and the kindness and caring radiating from them made the tight feeling in his chest start to ease.

"Who you were born to wasn't *your* fault," she said emphatically.

He heard the trace of anger in her voice, all on his behalf, and it made him feel lighter somehow, knowing finally someone cared about what had been done to him.

He pressed his fingers against the table before answering. "That would be a logical person's thought process, but according to my Aunt Becca, my father couldn't get over where I'd come from. When I was little, I remember wanting my father's attention so badly, and I couldn't understand why he ignored me and treated me like I was a leper. And when my mother got pregnant five years later and had my brother, Oliver, the fact that he was that miracle baby they never thought they'd have—and now I realize their *legitimate* child—made that separation between me and my father even worse."

He paused and drew a deep breath. "It was like I didn't even exist for him, and when he did acknowledge me, it was usually to point out some kind of failure or to put me down. But it was never that way with my brother. As Oliver got older, he'd take him fishing and leave me at home. He coached Oliver's soccer team and never bothered to come to any of my baseball games, and because my brother watched the disdainful way my father acted toward me, he did the same thing."

Tara winced but Jackson was more lost in his own thoughts. Now that everything was out in the open, he couldn't seem to stop the flood of memories from escaping. It was like a vein had burst open and all the toxic poison he'd been carrying around was finally spilling out, purging him of all the pain he'd kept buried for so long.

And Tara was there, listening, comforting him with her understanding silence.

"My mother died of breast cancer when I was ten, and after that, I swear I never felt so abandoned and alone and confused. I couldn't understand why my father treated me the way he did, and I spent years trying to be a good kid, doing everything I could to please him, to earn even an ounce of the attention he gave to Oliver, but it never made a difference." Looking back, Jackson could only imagine how pathetic his father thought he'd been in his attempts to gain his approval. His affection.

"Jackson . . . " Tara's husky voice was filled with heartache for him. "I'm so sorry."

A sharp exhale escaped him as he scrubbed a hand along his jaw. He forced an indifferent smile, trying to eliminate the oppressive mood that hung in the air now that he'd tainted it with his depressing backstory. "It is what it is, right?"

She nodded, but the warmth and caring never left her gaze. "Now that you know about where you came from, have you tried talking to your father?"

"No." The word came out harsh and unyielding. "We've been estranged for years. That relationship is irreparable." Initially, he'd thought about confronting his father about the past, but Jackson knew there was nothing Paul Stone could say or do that would allow Jackson to forgive him for the emotional and mental abuse his father had put him through. There was no remorse on his father's end, so what would it resolve?

"I get it," she said, her reply giving him the impression that she'd had challenging relationships of her own that hadn't ended well, either. He hoped that someday she'd trust him enough to confide in him as he'd done with her.

"Some things . . . some people, won't ever change," she murmured. "Sometimes, it's for the best to just move on."

Jackson would like to believe he had moved on from his father's narrow-minded ignorance. And now he was more than ready to move on from this dismal conversation.

He crumpled his napkin and stuffed it into the empty paper bag. "Jesus, for a first date, that was way too depressing," he joked.

"No, it wasn't." She smiled at him as she added her napkin to the trash, too. "I'm glad you told me. Your brothers should know how you grew up, that it wasn't as easy or perfect as they might think."

He shook his head and sighed. "I don't think they want to hear the truth."

"Maybe they're not *ready* to hear it yet," she qualified. "They're not going to ignore you forever, and I think they just need some time to come around."

She sounded so optimistic that he decided to remain hopeful, as well. He had nothing left to lose. "I suppose time is the one thing I have plenty of."

"Exactly," she agreed with a bright smile as she stood, then looked down at her hands with a grimace. "I need to wash my sticky fingers before we go."

He watched her walk down a short hallway, his gaze drawn to the sensual sway of her hips and that pert ass he knew would be a distinct part of his fantasies when he went to bed tonight. Once she disappeared into a side door, he collected their empty paper cups and threw all of their trash away, then waited for her to return.

As he stood there, he realized that over the course of their conversation, that constricting feeling in his chest that he'd been carrying around the past few weeks, since he'd learned of his illegal adoption, had decreased. It no longer felt like a crushing weight, and even some of his anger toward the situation had abated. He wasn't a guy who was big on spilling his guts and airing dirty laundry, but then again, he'd never had someone who'd been so focused on him and genuinely interested in what he had to say that wasn't work-related.

In an hour's time in Tara's company, he'd given her more insight into his past, had revealed insecurities he'd carried around with him for most of his life, and laid out the entire foundation of his not-so-great childhood. Trusting someone didn't come quickly or easily for him, yet he'd let his barriers slip with her, had shared deeply emotional things with Tara that he'd never even told his ex-wife because she'd never asked. And he'd never offered because a part of him feared she'd find him lacking, just as his father had.

And fuck if that hadn't happened anyway. In the end, he'd realized that Collette had her own agenda when it came to their marriage. She'd been enamored with his wealth, his success, and his social connections in Chicago. After two short years of marriage, everything had lost its luster, including him.

But there was something about Tara that *got him*, in a way that no one else ever had. Maybe it was her connection to the Kincaid brothers and being privy to their turbulent past that made it easy for her to understand all the pain and grief their birth mother had caused, for his siblings, and for him, each in different ways. Or maybe it was those secrets of her own that he'd glimpsed that allowed Tara to relate so well to his predicament.

Whatever the reason, he wasn't ready to let her go just yet.

Chapter Five

TARA LET THE cool water rush over her hands as she glanced up at her reflection in the bathroom mirror, thinking how so much of what Jackson had revealed about himself had resonated with her. She might not have been illegally adopted, but her childhood had been equally rocky, and it had led to an addiction to drugs as a way to escape the pain of never being able to live up to her parents'—her father's especially—expectations. Learning of their daughter's substance abuse had only compounded their disgrace and shame and condemnation, which in turn had given Tara even more of a reason to keep those opiates in her system to numb her upheaval of emotions.

Instead of getting her the help she desperately needed, they'd kicked her out of the house and cut her off completely, because her strict, hard-ass of a father had zero tolerance for disobedience and no patience for mistakes or a lapse in judgment. And her mother . . . well, she'd been too timid and meek to contradict her husband's orders. Even when Tara and her boyfriend at the time had ended up in the hospital for an overdose, and Michael had died of cardiac arrest that morning as a result of their excessive bingeing, her parents had never acknowledged her near-death experience.

There had been no one to console her through the devastation of losing someone she'd cared deeply for. No family to help her through her overwhelming grief and survivor's guilt she'd struggled with. Even Michael's wealthy family had blamed Tara for his death, and his sister, Brynn, had spewed such hate-filled words the last time Tara had seen her that Tara had wanted to curl up and die herself.

It had been the darkest, most terrifying time of her life, and she'd never felt so isolated and afraid. Or abandoned.

Clay Kincaid had changed all that. Once she'd left rehab clean and sober, he'd offered her a job and a chance to get it right. From the moment she started working for him, she'd felt the support of his brothers and the rest of the employees at Kincaid's. They were all like family to each other, including Katrina, Samantha, and Sarah—the amazing women who were now a part of each brother's life.

Other than that small circle of people, Tara was a loner. She'd spent the past six years focused on her job, going to school, studying, and working through the guilt of Michael's death with a therapist. She knew the self-blame would never go away completely, that sense of loss, but at least she'd learned to deal with the pain without reverting to those prescription drugs that had dulled her senses.

She exhaled a sigh and glanced away from her image in the mirror as she lathered up a dollop of liquid soap over her hands. Everything about that time in her life had left her cautious, careful, and guarded. A part of her was afraid of letting go again, of allowing herself to feel deeply for someone, especially a man. She held herself back out of fear of not being good enough, of being tainted by a past filled with disgrace and shame, and therefore she was alone . . . and lonely. And that solitude was most evident when she witnessed the intimate, loving relationships that Clay, Mason, and Levi had managed to find for themselves. With them all paired off, she sometimes felt like the odd woman out.

She'd dated a few times over the years since leaving rehab, but nothing had ever panned out. There had never been any sparks worth pursuing, and while the guys she'd gone out with had been more than eager to make it all about a casual hookup, it had never felt right for her. Therefore, she'd been deliberately celibate for the past six years. She and her battery-operated boyfriend were on really good terms. He gave her as many orgasms as she wanted and expected nothing in return.

It had been the perfect arrangement without any emotional complications, until Jackson had walked into Kincaid's a week ago and ignited a desire that only burned hotter and brighter each time she saw him. It was as though he'd flipped a switch inside her and had awakened all those erogenous zones that had lain dormant for so long. And the few times he'd touched her, she'd experienced a jolt of need that made her crave more of him.

There was no denying that she wanted him to caress her body until she melted and moaned, which she suspected wouldn't take much. She wanted those full, sensual lips sliding against hers, hard and demanding and hungry. And while he was at it, she wouldn't mind his mouth on her breasts, sucking her nipples, and his tongue delving between her thighs. That was definitely something her vibrator wasn't capable of.

She turned off the cool water and reached for a paper towel as those shameless thoughts of Jackson managed to do what all her previous dates had failed to accomplish—make her wet and aroused and aching for the feel of a real cock thrusting deep inside her.

She bit her bottom lip to keep her moan from escaping and came to a solid conclusion based on their mutual chemistry. Jackson Stone was exactly what she needed to finally end her six-year dry spell. He was gorgeous and sexy and pure temptation. Lean and lightly muscled in all the right places—the T-shirt and jeans he'd worn tonight showed off his toned physique more than his suit from the prior week had—he had a body made for pleasuring a woman, and she had no doubt he'd leave her thoroughly satisfied, in every way.

And she wouldn't mind returning the favor, making sure she had the opportunity to explore his hard, hot body, too—with her fingers, her lips, her tongue.

Yeah, she wanted all that. Wanted *him*.

Now that she'd made the decision to go for it—or rather, go for Jackson—a thrilling anticipation took up residence in her, one she embraced because it felt like forever since her body had been this attuned to a man.

She didn't fool herself into believing that she was the type of woman who'd fit into the affluent life he'd created for himself on a long-term basis—not that she was looking for that kind of commitment. She was hardly cultured or sophisticated, and her past drug addiction and overdose were like a scarlet letter on her chest, but she could at least enjoy Jackson for a while. Too many years had passed her by since she'd done something for herself, for no other reason than she wanted, *needed*, to feel desired again.

Tara smiled at the woman staring back at her as a sudden flutter of nerves swirled in her belly. God, she hoped she hadn't forgotten how to seduce a man. She was so out of practice, abysmally so, but if she didn't make some kind of attempt, the opportunity might pass her by, and she didn't want to look back and have regrets and wish she'd taken that chance.

She wanted to take a chance with Jackson. Sexually speaking, that was. Nothing complicated. Just sex for the sake of pleasure. This gorgeous guy who'd already admitted he wanted to do dirty, bad things to her was the perfect man to end her six-year drought.

Bolstering her courage, she walked back out of the restroom. Jackson was leaning against the table they'd eaten their donuts at, waiting for her return. She took a moment to appreciate the way the soft fabric of his T-shirt stretched across his well-defined chest and how the short sleeves hugged his strong biceps. His fingers were tucked into the front pockets of his jeans, drawing her gaze to the way the denim molded to the soft bulge beneath the zipper. His legs were crossed casually at the ankles, and when she finally traversed her way back up to his handsome face that was dusted with just the right amount of sexy stubble, one of his dark eyebrows was raised and a wicked smile tugged at his mouth.

Heat and awareness thrummed through her. She ought to be embarrassed at getting caught but decided that shying away from their physical connection wouldn't get her anywhere. So, she lifted an eyebrow of her own in a shameless challenge as she approached him.

"Were you just checking me out?" His voice was a low, rumbling tease.

She laughed lightly and played along. Flirtatious ribbing she could do. "You stared at my ass back at the bar, so fair is fair."

"Just for the sake of honesty and full disclosure, I've stared at your enticing ass a *whole* lot," he admitted as he pushed away from the table and guided her toward the door with one hand at the base of her spine. Then he leaned in close and added oh so sinfully, "Thought about smacking it a few times, too."

Her breath caught when he subtly caressed his large palm over the curve of her bottom, and for a brief second, she wondered if he was going to follow through on his admission—and oh, God, the thought had her quivering in anticipation—but instead his hand fell away as he opened the door for her.

As she walked past him with a murmured "thank you," she looked up and caught his gaze. The twinkle in his dark, chocolate-brown eyes conveyed a distinct message there was no misinterpreting: *two can play your game.*

Oh, he was definitely having fun toying with her, and the fact that they were on the same page when it came to their attraction only solidified her confidence. Made her feel naughty and sexy and just a little bit risqué.

As they walked toward their cars, she gave him a sidelong glance. After everything she'd just learned about him, and the things she knew to be true and had already seen for herself, like his decency and his integrity, she posed a question that added to the lighthearted mood between them.

"So, Jackson . . . I can't decide if you're a saint like your brother Clay or if you're more the sinner type."

He slipped his hand into hers, grabbing it securely in his grip as he brought her thumb to his mouth and bit on the tip, just sharp enough to make her gasp in surprise. That nip also injected her entire body with lust.

There was nothing saint-like about the heat in his eyes as he held her gaze. "Nobody's ever called me a saint, and just because you might look at me and see Clay because we're identical twins, I can assure you that doesn't mean we share that trait."

Actually, when she looked at Jackson now, she no longer saw him as a cookie-cutter version of his brother as she had at first. Now that she knew him better, she saw him for a kind, caring individual struggling to come to terms with the bombshell he'd been dealt upon learning about his illegal adoption while trying to make amends with his brothers. This man walking beside her made Tara's heart ache for everything that had been stolen from him, for the appalling childhood he'd endured, and how badly he wanted his siblings to accept him as one of their own.

But she didn't say any of that, because she didn't want to dampen their enjoyable banter with something so serious.

She grinned up at him as they reached her vehicle. "So, what you're saying, then, is that you fall into the sinner category?"

He released her hand and backed her up against the driver's-side door, then braced his palms on either side of her shoulders, caging her between her car and his big, solid frame. He wasn't touching her anywhere, yet she tingled all over. His body remained mere inches away, tempting and teasing her, and she was suddenly dying to feel it pressed hard against hers.

"Let's put it this way, sweetheart," he drawled in a

tone of voice that was infused with pure, illicit sex. "If you knew all the filthy, explicit things I've fantasized about doing to you, there would be no doubts in your mind that I'm a sinner in all the ways that matter."

Her breathing deepened, and she licked her bottom lip, nearly groaning when his gaze followed the slow slide of her tongue. Except for the two of them, it was deserted in the back parking area and dimly lit. They were standing between both of their cars, which blocked them from view from anyone driving by.

She placed her hand on his hips, wishing it was his bare skin beneath her fingers and not the fabric of his shirt. "Tell me all the ways you want to sin with me," she whispered, needing to hear every indecent detail.

He moved his hands from her car, pressing them gently against the sides of her face and tipping her head back so he was looking directly into her eyes. "Sin number one revolves around this sweet, beautiful mouth of yours. I've dreamed about kissing it, wondered too many times to count how you'd taste deep inside." His thumb skimmed along her damp bottom lip, tugging provocatively on the full flesh. "But that's a mild fantasy compared to the one I have of fisting my hands in your hair and pushing you to your knees in front of me. Want to know what happens after that?"

Those legs he just spoke of weakened, and she was grateful for the support of the vehicle behind her. Mimicking his words, Jackson's fingers had already found their way into her hair, and she felt a distinct tug against her scalp as he wrapped the long strands around his hand. She felt the power and control in his grip, saw the glow of hunger in his eyes as he waited for her to answer.

A shiver stole through her. "Yes, I want to know everything." Her voice was so filled with passion she hardly recognized it as her own.

He leaned into her, the stiff length of his cock nestling at the crux of her thighs as he tipped her head to the side and brought his stubbled cheek to hers so that he could whisper huskily into her ear. "Sin number two is all about having your soft lips wrapped tight around my dick as you suck me, and your hot mouth taking me so fucking deep I hit the back of your throat."

Between the arousing scratch of his facial hair against her skin, his hips doing a slow grind against hers, and his uncensored descriptions, all she could do was close her eyes and moan. Her nipples were so tight they hurt, and there was no mistaking the slick moisture dampening her panties or the way her sex pulsed with need. She'd never been so turned on before, had never been so overwhelmed with such wild, uncontrollable desire for a man.

His warm breath tickled her ear as he untangled his fingers from her hair and smoothed his palms down the sides of her body, bypassing her swollen, aching breasts, much to her disappointment. His big hands traced along the curve of her hips—God, she hated the clothing between them—then slid around to her backside and grabbed and squeezed her ass.

He bent slightly, allowing his hands to smooth lower so that they were now gripping the backs of her thighs. Bracing her against the car, he lifted both of her legs, securing them on either side of his hips until she was forced to wrap them tight around his waist. She instinctively locked her ankles at the small of his back, and her hands clung to his shoulders, holding on, as he rocked every part of his body against hers. The friction of his erection along her sex had her writhing against that solid column of flesh, seeking some kind of relief to the relentless throb between her thighs.

"Jackson . . . " She wasn't sure if his name on her lips was out of shock or a plea for him to end the sensual torment he was putting her through.

He ignored her attempt to get his attention. "You ready for sin number three, baby?" he growled into her ear, but didn't wait for her reply. Not that any response was needed considering the wanton way she was rubbing against him like a cat in heat.

"I've thought about spreading your legs wide and burying my mouth between your creamy thighs. I've imagined licking your pussy until you come so fucking hard you see stars." He flicked his tongue against her neck, then grazed his teeth along that same patch of sensitive skin, making her shiver. "Then I'd roll you over and put you on your hands and knees so I could mark you as mine with a nice pink handprint on your soft ass before driving into you from behind until your second orgasm milks me dry."

He had her so worked up she was panting, her skin hot and flushed and her pussy screaming for some kind of relief from all his verbal foreplay. He lifted his head from her throat and lightly brushed his lips across hers.

"Do you want to sin with me, Tara?" he asked against her mouth.

Head spinning, throat tight, she somehow managed to answer. "God, yes. *Please*."

He finally crushed his lips to hers, devouring her like a man starved for the taste of her, thrusting his tongue deep inside as his raw, guttural groan of need vibrated throughout her entire body. She threaded her fingers through the soft strands of his hair as his mouth demanded her acquiescence, and she let him take complete control of the kiss, succumbing to every ounce of pleasure he gave her.

He shifted one of his legs so that his thigh supported her bottom, freeing his hands for other more sensual pursuits. He tugged the hem of her work shirt from her jeans, and she moaned her gratitude when his fingers touched her bare stomach, then glided up her rib cage. She was wearing a bra, but that didn't stop him from enveloping her breasts in the scorching heat of his palms or dissuade his thumbs from flicking and teasing the impossibly hard tips of her nipples through the thin, lacy fabric. Breathing took a back seat to pure sensation as the ache between her thighs gathered force with every slow, searing stroke of his shaft against her core.

She squirmed to get closer. Clenched her thighs around his hips to increase the pressure right where she needed it the most. Even confined beneath the zipper of his jeans, there was no denying his cock was thick and huge, more so than the vibrator she'd grown used to, which would now forever pale in comparison. She imagined all that solid male heat working its way inside her, inch by delectable inch. Envisioned him filling her with the breath-stealing force he'd just described and without any restraint holding him back from taking what he ultimately wanted . . .

And then, it all abruptly ended as Jackson tore his mouth from hers and cursed beneath his breath. Despite her weak protest, he untangled their limbs and gradually released her so that she was standing on her own two feet again. A little unsteady, but his hands on her waist helped.

"We can't do this here," he said in a gruff voice, but the frustration etching his expression, the un-quenched desire, was just as keen as her own.

Her passion-hazed mind cleared, their surround-ings came back into focus, and her skin flushed when she realized what she'd nearly allowed in a public place.

"And if I take you home right now, neither one of us will get any sleep because I will fuck you for hours," he added in a low, heated tone that was filled with regret. "Which means I won't be worth shit at a very important meeting I have at work in the morning."

The only thing she could manage was an agreeable nod.

"I want to see you again." He tenderly brushed unruly tendrils of her hair away from her cheek, his gaze searching hers, bright with determination. "I *need* to see you again."

She understood that same strong urge to be with him again, too. Not just to finish what they'd started tonight but because she really liked the way he made her feel. More vibrant and alive than she had since losing Michael. Like she finally had something exciting to look forward to other than the mundane existence she'd lived for so many years.

"I work Thursday and Friday night," she said and, for the first time ever, hated that she worked the evening shift, because it conflicted with his nine-to-five schedule.

He tipped his head. "Saturday?" he asked hopefully.

"I'm off." And then she remembered *why* she wasn't on the schedule for that night. Because Clay had essentially ordered her to take the day off for a party being thrown in her honor.

"So, how about we go out on a real date then?" he suggested.

Tara didn't respond immediately and instead considered her options. She couldn't very well blow off her friends and the barbeque they'd planned to celebrate her finally getting her degree. But she could invite Jackson to join her, which would also force Clay,

Mason, and Levi to deal with the reality of having a brother who was a decent guy and not the threat they believed him to be. Maybe, hopefully, having them all in a casual setting would make it easier for them to get to know one another better.

She reached out and placed her hands on his chest, because she liked touching him and she also hoped that the connection between the two of them would help sway him. "So . . . Samantha, Katrina, and Sarah are throwing me a graduation party on Saturday at Clay's house," she said quickly. "Come with me."

His body tensed, and he stared at her as if she'd just grown a third eye. "You're kidding, right?"

She shook her head. "No, I'm completely serious."

His frown increased, his dark brown eyes reflecting his apprehension. "Tara, my brothers don't want to have anything to do with me. What makes you think they're going to be okay with me crashing a party I wasn't invited to?"

"You wouldn't be crashing because *I'm* inviting you, as my guest," she said with an encouraging smile. "It's my party and I want you there. Doesn't that count for anything?"

He scrubbed a hand over his clenched jaw, clearly torn. He hadn't said yes, but he hadn't flat out refused her, either, and that's what Tara concentrated on.

"I'd really like you to be there, and I honestly think it would help your cause if you met Samantha, Katrina, and Sarah, because they're the ones who can sway the guys. Really."

He didn't look totally convinced, but the small, wry smile curving the corner of his mouth told her he was considering her invitation. "You don't ask for much, do you?"

She shrugged. "The very worst that could happen is that they tell you to leave, though I'm pretty sure they won't. They might be acting like closed-minded idiots right now, but you all have to start somewhere, right?"

Tara had no idea why the brothers hadn't reached out to Jackson since meeting him. Their distrust of outsiders was a typical reaction for the three men, and she could only assume that they were still trying to process Jackson's existence. Sure, they might be surprised to see him at her party, possibly even wary at first, but she was determined to give *all* of them a nudge in the right direction. And hopefully, with Samantha, Katrina, and Sarah as buffers, their significant others' cool demeanor toward Jackson would start to thaw.

"So, what do you say?" she asked persuasively, knowing he was close to agreeing. "Do you want to pick me up at three on Saturday?"

He released a heavy breath and finally nodded, clearly wanting what she was offering. "Yeah, I'd like that. A lot."

She grinned triumphantly as she took her cell phone from her purse. "What's your phone number so I can text you my number and address," she said before he had too much time to think about his decision and have second thoughts.

He gave her his contact information and she typed it in, then immediately sent him a message with her street address, which also gave him her cell number. Once that was done, she dropped her phone back into her handbag, then poked him playfully in the chest.

"Technically, this is a date, so no backing out," she said impudently.

He caught her hand before she could pull it away and flicked his tongue along the pulse point in her wrist, his gaze hot and seductive and amused. "Or what?" he murmured.

That quickly, that easily, a renewed longing sizzled through her. "If you cancel, there'll be no sinning for you, that's what," she replied with sass.

"Damn," he muttered with a feigned frown. "You drive one hell of a hard bargain."

She laughed lightly. "It's called an incentive. Just keep your eye on the prize, Mr. Stone, and don't forget how Saturday night is going to end."

He grinned at her. "And how's that?"

God, he was so charming, with just enough bad boy thrown in for good measure, which made him incredibly difficult to resist. But then again, she'd already decided that she was going to enjoy him, the flirting, the sex . . . whatever this was between them.

Leaning toward him, she placed a kiss on the corner of his mouth, then whispered in his ear, "Saturday night will end any way you want it to," she promised.

He pulled back slightly, so she couldn't miss the

carnal look in his eyes, the salacious expression flashing across his bold, masculine features. "There's always sin number four, where you're sitting astride my cock as I—"

She quickly covered his mouth and groaned, her body and senses already on overload and on the verge of spontaneously combusting from all his dirty talk. "You're seriously killing me."

He pulled her hand away, a smirk on his lips. "What I plan to do to you won't kill you, but it might just make you scream with pleasure. In fact, that's what I'll be aiming for. Numerous times."

Tara didn't think she could be any more aroused, but Jesus, the man was lethal and every sexual fantasy she'd ever had. Saturday seemed like a lifetime away, but she was pretty damn sure that sinning with Jackson Stone was going to be worth the wait.

Chapter Six

JACKSON WALKED INTO The Popped Cherry, the trendy bar in downtown Chicago where he'd promised to meet up with his good friend, Wes Sinclair, after work. It was nearly six thirty on a Friday night, and the place was already packed. As he made his way through the crowd, he glanced over at the bar as Tate Morrison, one of the owners of the place, glanced up from the bottle of vodka he'd just picked up.

"Hey, man. How's it going?" Tate greeted him without breaking stride on the cocktail he was mixing.

"Good." Jackson stopped next to a barstool where Tate's significant other, Logan Mitchell, was sitting, and shook the other man's hand. The dark-haired, good-looking guy was a lawyer at Mitchell and Madison in the city, and his half brother, Cole, had been counsel on Jackson's divorce three years ago. They'd remained good friends since then.

Jackson casually leaned an arm on the counter next to Logan. "How are things at the office?"

"Busy." Logan took a quick drink of his gin and tonic. "Which is always a good thing, so I'm not complaining."

Jackson raised a brow. "Can't be too busy if you can still find time to harass Tate at work."

Behind the black-framed glasses Logan wore, his blue eyes gleamed with humor. "Being part owner of the joint, it's my job to make sure I keep Tate in line."

Tate scoffed at his boyfriend's arrogant comment and shook his head. "Don't worry, Jackson. I definitely put Logan in his place at home. Frequently."

Logan smirked, though there was no mistaking the affection in his voice when he spoke. "And you do it oh so well."

"Don't you forget it." Tate gave Logan a flirty grin before shifting his gaze back to Jackson. "Bushmills, neat?"

Jackson nodded. "That would be great. Thank you."

As Tate poured his drink, Jackson glanced around the place, searching for Wes. As he did so, he couldn't help but compare the contemporary, modern design of The Popped Cherry, which catered more toward corporate clientele, to Clay's simple and modest bar. The two establishments were night and day in comparison, and as much as Jackson enjoyed this place, there was something about Kincaid's that made him feel as though he fit in and belonged there.

It was a ridiculous notion considering his brothers' cool reception had made him feel more like an outsider than someone they were eager to establish any kind of a relationship with. No, it was Tara who'd made him feel welcome and accepted from the first moment they'd met, in a way that had eluded him for most of his life. She was the one supporting his efforts to connect with his siblings, not because she expected something in return but because she genuinely cared about the Kincaid brothers and wanted to be sure they didn't miss out on the opportunity to get to know Jackson.

For a man who'd experienced very little kindness and caring throughout his life, her compassion and understanding toward the situation, and with him, was something he cherished. It remained to be seen whether it had been a smart or stupid decision on his part to agree to accompany Tara to Clay's house tomorrow afternoon for her graduation party. He had no idea what kind of reception to expect, but he wanted this time with his brothers badly enough to risk their wrath by showing up.

Tate set his glass of whiskey on the counter, and Jackson pulled a twenty out of his wallet to pay for the drink. "Have either of you seen Wes?" he asked the two men.

Logan nodded to the right of Jackson. "He's right over there, doing what he does best."

Jackson didn't have to turn around to know that Wes was most likely surrounded by a selection of attentive, willing, beautiful females. The man was a shameless flirt who enjoyed women. Unfortunately for the ladies he hooked up with, he was also a notorious heartbreaker and didn't do serious relationships.

A wry grin tugged up the corner of Jackson's mouth. "Are panties hitting the floor?"

Logan chuckled. "Not yet, but he definitely has a few of them heading in that direction."

"Then I'd better go and save him from himself." Jackson picked up his drink and nodded to each of the men. "You two have a good evening."

He walked toward where Logan had indicated, and sure enough, Wes was in his element, surrounded by three perky blondes who were all vying for his attention and hanging on every word he spoke. The man was too damn good-looking for his own well-being, with that bad-boy air about him that had every woman believing she'd be the one to tame him. *Yeah, good luck with that.*

Wes caught sight of Jackson as he approached, but since Jackson had no desire to make idle conversation with any of those women, he strolled toward a high-top table that a couple had just vacated and claimed it for himself. He slid onto one of the barstools and waited for Romeo to come and join him. As he sat there, the cell phone in his pocket vibrated, and he pulled it out to see who'd texted him.

Tara: *I just want to make sure that we're still on for tomorrow?*

Just seeing her name put a stupid smile on his face. Damn, it had been a long time since any woman had given him a genuine reason to feel lighthearted and happy, which happened every time he'd talked or texted with Tara since their donut date two nights ago.

They'd spent over two hours chatting on the phone last night after she'd gotten off of work—surprisingly, she'd called him—conversing mostly about him and his job as an architect since she didn't like to talk about herself. He would have liked to have learned more about her and that past she was so vague about, but he knew how difficult it was to let someone in, to open up and reveal painful things when you weren't ready. He hoped she'd eventually realize that she could trust him. It was shocking to him that he could feel so much for her so quickly.

He texted back, keeping things light and fun. *Which part of tomorrow are you referring to? The party or the sinning?*

She quickly replied. *You can't have one without the other.*

He chuckled, enjoying her sassy retort. *Well, technically you can, but since I'm not willing to forego the sinning, I'll be right on time to pick you up for the party.*

Good. There was a break in the text, then those three bubbles appeared that told him another comment was on its way. *I'm really looking forward to seeing you.*

There was something intimate about the words despite them being so casual. Something that made his heart beat a little faster because it meant she'd missed him. Though they'd only known each other a little over a week and a half, he knew they were both feeling more than just a basic attraction. He was so drawn to Tara, the connection he felt when he was with her was like nothing else he'd ever experienced with a woman, and he didn't want to take it, or her, for granted.

He typed a response. *I can't wait to see you tomorrow, too.*

He figured she was at work, because she didn't text back, and he hated that a part of him was disappointed that her attention had been diverted elsewhere. Grinning to himself, he decided to leave her a surprise text for when she checked her phone later in the evening. A little something for her to look forward to tomorrow night after the party, when they were finally alone and he had her all to himself.

Sin number four . . . driving my cock into you hard and deep while watching you pinch your nipples and finger your pussy until we both come.

Yeah, that ought to give her a nice, sexy fantasy to think about.

A few minutes later, Wes took the seat across from Jackson and set his drink on the table. "Hey, Mr. Unsociable. I could have introduced you to a sure thing back there."

"Thanks, but I'm not interested." He was way more discriminate than his friend, and always had been. Then again, right now there was only one woman who piqued his attention, and that was Tara.

He didn't see that ending anytime soon . . . as long as Tara maintained equal interest in him.

"You've been quiet the past week and a half and haven't returned my calls," Wes pointed out, even as his gaze strayed to a table to the left of them where three women were sitting. "Everything okay?"

Those calls had been all about having a drink together, and tonight was the first evening since finding out about his illegal adoption that Jackson was clear-minded enough to meet up with his friend. "I just have some things going on that I'm trying to deal with."

"Work?" Wes guessed.

"No, work is fine." Jackson absently turned his glass in a circle on the napkin it was sitting on. "Just some personal shit I've been trying to figure out."

Wes raised an inquisitive brow. "Care to elaborate on that?"

Jackson met Wes's earnest gaze. For the most part, Wes was easygoing and didn't take much seriously, but it was times like this that reminded Jackson what a good friend Wes had been after Jackson's wife's affair and their subsequent divorce. He'd known Wes for over five years now. The other man was a luxury real estate agent, and they'd met at a business function. A few weeks after that, Wes had sold Jackson his first condo on Lake Shore Drive, and a strong friendship had built from there.

The only people Jackson had told about his illegal adoption had been his brothers and Tara, and since he was hoping that eventually he'd form some kind of relationship with his siblings, there was no sense keeping the truth to himself.

He took a long swallow of his whiskey and proceeded to tell Wes everything—how his aunt had decided that Jackson had a right to know about his past, and all the ugly details of being sold for drug money and how his father had essentially ignored him his entire life because of who and what Jackson was, and about finally contacting his brothers about his existence, only to be shut out once again.

"Jesus," Wes said once Jackson was finished with his story. "That's some heavy-duty shit."

"Tell me about it," he said, his tone derisive. "So yeah, I've been a little distracted lately."

"I totally get it." Wes's gaze once again wandered to the other table before returning to Jackson. "And just for the record, your brothers sound like assholes."

Jackson laughed abruptly. He'd had a lot of time to think about his siblings' reactions to him. A part of him understood their initial caution, but he was having a difficult time discerning why they hadn't bothered to contact him since that meeting—unless they truly didn't want to have anything to do with him. It was a notion that Jackson hated to think about and refused to accept.

"They're not assholes." Okay, maybe Mason had been a bit of an asshole, Jackson corrected in his head. "They're just wary."

Wes frowned at him. "You said one of the brothers was your twin. What's there to be wary about?"

"They don't know anything about me, so I'm assuming they just need time to get used to the idea of having another brother that came as a complete surprise." He was trying to give the Kincaid siblings the benefit of the doubt, though it didn't appear that they were returning the favor. "Tomorrow night, one of the bartenders who works for Clay is bringing me to a party they're having for her. There's no telling how that's going to go down, but I figure it's worth trying to break the ice."

A slow smile tugged at the corner of Wes's mouth as he raised an inquisitive brow. "Her?"

Out of everything Jackson had just said, that's what he'd latched onto? Knowing his friend would endlessly hound him, Jackson told Wes what he wanted to hear. "Her name is Tara."

Wes tapped his fingers on the table. "And how is it that you know Tara well enough that she invited you to this party, hmmm?"

"I met her the night I went to the bar. We've talked a few times since then." Jackson shrugged. "She's close to the Kincaid brothers and wants to help initiate some kind of reunion between the four of us."

Wes nodded, but once again Jackson noticed that he was distracted by the women at the other table, or rather, one of the ladies. His gaze was riveted to the brunette who was facing him, but she wouldn't so much as glance his way.

"What is up with you and that woman at the other

table?" Jackson finally asked. He was surprised that someone so prim-and-proper-looking had captured Wes's attention, when he was a guy who'd always gone for the fast-and-easy type. "You keep staring at her like you're a stalker."

"You know my business partner, Connor Prescott?" Wes asked.

Jackson nodded. "Yes." The guy flipped a lot of the luxury homes that Wes bought that were in dire need of updates and renovations.

"Well, that's his little sister, Natalie. I've known her since I was ten, and we've always had a love hate relationship."

Another glance at the brunette told Jackson that she was totally blowing Wes off. "Looks more like hate to me at the moment."

"She's just acting a bit haughty because she sold a house right out from under me." Wes shrugged. "Doesn't happen often, so she's a little pleased with herself right now."

"So why do you keep looking at her like you want to hook up with her?"

"Well, she is kind of hot . . . in an uptight kind of way."

Jackson laughed. "And off-limits?"

"Yeah." He exhaled a sigh as Natalie continued to ignore him, even though the friends she was with clearly saw Wes looking her way. "Connor would castrate me if I so much as touched her that way. But damn, between you and me, when she plays hard to get, she's so fucking tempting I want to toss her over my shoulder and take her somewhere and do dirty things to her."

Jackson bit back an amused grin. "She doesn't look that in to you."

"Oh, trust me, beneath that indifference is an attraction she's been fighting just as much as I have," Wes said. "I love a good challenge, so I'm pretty damn sure her days of ignoring me are limited."

"You're such an arrogant asshole, Sinclair."

"It's called *confidence*, Stone," his friend retorted. "Or maybe it's been too damn long since you've been in the game and you've forgotten how it's played?"

The thing was, Jackson had never played those games, ever. He'd always been an all-in kind of guy when it came to women and relationships. Or he had been in the past, before his ex-wife had burned and scarred him. Since then, he hadn't allowed himself to form any emotional attachments to the women he'd gone out with. It had been all about sex, and they'd all known his intentions up front.

It had taken him three years to find a woman he wanted for more than just a bed partner and a physical release. He was attracted to Tara, and there was no denying he wanted to fuck her a dozen different ways. But he instinctively knew that she'd already gotten under his skin just based on how he felt when he was around her. Lighter. Understood. Like a man who might be given a second chance at something real and, dare he say, lasting?

Was that thought process crazy after only knowing Tara a short time? Absolutely. Was he setting himself up for a hard fall considering her connection and loyalty to Clay, Mason and Levi?

Possibly.

He realized it was a risk he was willing to take.

TARA KNEW SHE'D made the right decision asking Jackson to accompany her to her graduation celebration party, but that knowledge didn't stop the flutters of anticipation from swirling in her belly as she waited for him to arrive to pick her up.

That nervousness was twofold. One, she hadn't told the Kincaid brothers that she was bringing Jackson because she didn't want to give them the opportunity to turn her down, so there was no telling what kind of reaction she and Jackson would receive when they arrived. And the second reason for those nerves was Jackson himself and the fact that she was excited to see him, spend time with him, and end the night with just the two of them all alone . . . *sinning*.

Good-bye to six years of celibacy and hello, dirty, sexy pleasure.

She grinned to herself as she left her bedroom and headed into the small living room in the house she'd bought on her own a few years ago. The two-bedroom one-story wasn't much, but it was hers and no one could take it away. She'd always have somewhere to live, and it gave her a sense of security because she knew all too well what it was like *not* to have a place to call home. She'd vowed long ago she'd never let that happen to her again.

The doorbell chimed right on time, and when she opened the door and saw Jackson standing there looking so devastatingly gorgeous, the giddy sensation rippling through her intensified. He was wearing black jeans and a dark purple collared shirt, but it was the seductive smile on his lips and the heat glimmering in his dark brown eyes as he looked at *her* with a slow, appraising look that had a warm flush of delight sweeping across her cheeks.

"Hi, beautiful," he murmured, his voice a low, husky rumble that did crazy things to her insides.

"Hi yourself, handsome." She sounded breathless and besotted—exactly how he made her feel. "Let me grab my purse and I'm good to go."

She didn't invite him in because she anticipated leaving right away. But Jackson clearly had other ideas. He entered on his own, closed the door, and closed the distance between them. Without hesitating, as if she already belonged to him, he walked right up to her and cupped her face in his big hands, gently pulling her toward him. She went willingly, mesmerized by the sudden hunger blazing in his eyes.

His thumb skimmed along her bottom lip, tugging the plump flesh so her mouth parted and opened for him on a soft, needy moan. "Three days without kissing you is too fucking long," he growled as he slid all ten fingers into her hair and tugged her head farther back.

The hands gripping her hair were firm and unrelenting, his confidence in taking what he wanted so damn arousing she was already beginning to melt. "I agree."

"I need a taste to hold me over until later tonight." He lowered his head, his teeth nipping softly, his tongue teasing flirtatiously, before he finally claimed her mouth completely.

She wrapped her arms around his neck, holding on to him as her soft lips melded to his firmer, more insistent ones, and all playfulness fled and hot, intense passion took over. His tongue pushed inside, swirling deep, not just tasting but exploring and feasting greedily. One hand untangled from her hair and glided down her side, along the curve of her waist, then smoothed over her jean-clad bottom. He squeezed her ass and drew her hips to his, making sure she felt how badly he wanted her—and there was no mistaking the thick column of flesh pressing relentlessly against her lower belly.

Her nipples tightened into hard points, and her entire body ached with wet, pulsing need. Every touch, every stroke swept her senses into overload and made her crave more of everything. More of him. And God, the man knew how to kiss. His lips were like magic, his delicious, decadent mouth an aphrodisiac she could easily get accustomed to. Or maybe she was already addicted, because as soon as he dragged his lips from hers, she went straight into withdrawal.

The hand clutching her ass slid upward, and he secured a strong arm around her waist, still holding her close. The fingers still in her hair tipped her head to the side, and she shivered as his damp lips slid down the side of her neck, exposed from where her top bared one shoulder.

"Are you sure I can't convince you to skip the party and finish what we just started?" he asked as he gently nuzzled the sensitive patch of skin below her lobe.

She moaned as his tongue traced a delectable pattern on her skin, making her imagine how it would feel between her legs, along her pulsing clit. The lust coursing through her veins sizzled and spread. How bad was it that she was seriously considering his suggestion?

She struggled to keep from slipping completely under his provocative spell, and it wasn't an easy feat. "You're such a bad influence."

Lifting his head, he captured her gaze as a wicked grin curved his seductive lips. "Is that a yes?" The rogue had the devilish nerve to look hopeful.

She laughed as she stepped out of his embrace, even though it was the last thing she wanted. With a reluctant sigh, he let her go.

"It would be rude for the guest of honor to not show up to her own celebration," she said, trying to keep her voice, and her own convictions, from wavering.

"Then we'd better go before I strip you naked and

have my way with you." He raked his hot gaze down the length of her, taking in the stiff nipples still pebbled against the fabric of her gray top before his bold, shameless eyes met hers again. "I don't think my brothers would appreciate you walking in late to your own party, looking like you'd just been thoroughly fucked."

That dirty mouth. Those indecent words. She groaned as her body flushed with desire and reckless temptation beckoned.

"We need to go," she said, attempting to sound stern. "*Now.*"

His chuckle was warm and deep and unapologetic as he walked toward the entry, and she followed. He opened the door, and as she passed through, he smacked her ass, hard enough for his handprint to sting through the material of her jeans.

She gasped and whirled around, gaping at him in shock, even as the tingling sensation turned into a slow burn of pleasure. "What was *that* for?"

He winked at her as a pleased, self-satisfied look crossed his gorgeous features. "Just giving you something to think about until we get back later."

Chapter Seven

TARA CAST A sidelong glance at Jackson as they walked side by side up the cobblestone walkway leading to Clay and Samantha's front porch. They'd left her house in a playful mood, but the closer they'd gotten to Clay's, the quieter Jackson had become. He was more subdued than she'd ever seen him, and she wanted to be sure that he was okay before they surprised everyone with his presence.

She lightly touched her fingers to the inside of his forearm, just to let him know that he had someone on his side no matter what happened once they entered the house. She wanted to hold his hand in a show of support, but she wasn't ready to make *that* kind of bold statement in front of the Kincaid brothers just yet. It was enough that she was surprising them by bringing Jackson. She didn't need to complicate matters by flaunting the fact that she was dating him.

"Nervous?" she asked as they climbed the four

steps leading to the front door.

"No." If he was lying, his steady voice gave nothing away, nor did his dark brown eyes when they met her gaze. "Are you?"

"Nope. Not even a little." She gave him a fearless smile that was an authentic and true reflection of her inner confidence. "I've known Clay, Mason, and Levi long enough to have learned that their growl is worse than their bite."

Jackson arched a dubious brow. "I don't know about that. Mason seemed pretty damn rabid."

She laughed but couldn't disagree. "It's mostly a defense mechanism. They're very protective when it comes to each other and the people they care about. Mason is just far more vocal about his approach."

She gave his arm one last squeeze and rang the doorbell, reminding herself that today's goal was to give all four of them the push they needed to connect beyond the strangers they were. If she accomplished that small task, she'd chalk it up to a victory.

Tara heard Samantha's feminine voice, along with Katrina's and Sarah's laughter as they approached the entry from the other side of the closed door. When it flew open, they all three shouted in unison, "Happy graduation!"

That animated greeting ebbed into silence as three pairs of eyes shifted to Jackson, standing by Tara's side. Their changing expressions were almost comical as they stared in shock at Clay's twin. Samantha's blue eyes were huge, Katrina's mouth had fallen open as though she couldn't find the words to speak, and Sarah blinked a few times as if she were seeing a mirage.

Without missing a beat, a charming smile eased across Jackson's mouth. "Hi, ladies," he said, amusement lacing his voice despite the reserve Tara detected in his body language.

His greeting was simple but effective and snapped all three women out of their stupor. Prim and proper Samantha was the first to react.

"Oh, my God, where are my manners!" she exclaimed apologetically as she opened the door wider for them to enter. "You must be Jackson. Come on in, please."

"Thank you," he replied with a polite nod, and followed Tara into the living room.

A sliver of relief allowed Tara to relax a bit. The Kincaid men had obviously told their women about their brother and Clay's twin. She wasn't sure what else they'd told the girls, but considering how excited they seemed to meet him, Tara was grateful that at least they were friendly and welcoming.

"It's so nice to meet you," Katrina gushed, shaking his hand with genuine warmth. She was the most eccentric one out of the group, with her purple-tipped hair and sleeve of colorful butterfly tattoos covering one arm.

"Yes, finally," Sarah added just as enthusiastically. "We were just telling the guys that we all wanted to meet you, and here you are. It was so great of Tara to bring you."

At the mention of Jackson being her guest, Katrina side-eyed Tara with sudden curiosity. Being out of Jackson's line of sight, the other woman raised a sassy brow that spoke louder than words, *how is it that you know Jackson so well that you're the one to bring him to the party? And what is going on between the two of you?*

Tara just smiled, giving nothing away. She had no doubt that Katrina would corner her later, probably along with Samantha and Sarah, to interrogate her when Jackson wasn't around.

"I can't get over how much you look like Clay." Samantha's creamy complexion blushed as the comment spilled out, and she absently stroked her hand over the small baby bump outlined beneath the cute top she was wearing. "I mean, I know you're twins, but it's just so strange to see . . . well, another Clay."

"Oh, I don't know," Katrina said, her tone teasing. "I think Jackson might be a better-looking version of Clay."

Samantha laughed lightly as she gave Jackson an impish look. "Sorry and no offense, but that's just not possible."

Jackson chuckled, looking completely at ease with the women. "No offense taken."

Sarah shook her head and chimed in as the peacemaker. "You two look identical, so I'd say you're equally handsome."

"Is the graduation girl finally here?" Clay's voice boomed from the kitchen area right before he walked into the living room. "Can't start the party without the guest of honor—"

His steps slowed, as did Mason's and Levi's, who'd been following Clay. All three men stopped and stared at Jackson, and the sudden strain in the room was nearly tangible. The silence was deafening.

What the hell was wrong with these guys? Annoyed with their behavior, Tara spoke up. "Don't be rude, boys," she said through gritted teeth, trying to sound pleasant when she was suddenly feeling very protective of Jackson. "Say hello to my *guest*."

Samantha gave Clay a pointed look, while Katrina jabbed Mason in the side with her elbow hard enough for him to grunt from the impact. The glare he aimed at Katrina didn't seem to faze his wife one bit. She was one of the few people who didn't put up with Mason's shit and could put him in his place.

Levi finally stepped forward, his demeanor reserved as he offered his hand to Jackson. "Good to see you." His tone, at least, was cordial.

"Likewise." The two men shook hands, followed by Clay and Mason, who were just as guarded with their acknowledgment.

Good God. There was no way Tara was going to spend the afternoon and evening with all this tension between the guys. Whatever their issue with Jackson, she was determined to find out. Starting right now.

"Samantha, would you mind taking Jackson out on the deck, get him a beer or something to drink while I talk to these guys?" Tara asked as she hitched her thumb toward the three brothers.

The other woman nodded in understanding. "Absolutely. Come on, Jackson. We want to know all about you."

Samantha, Katrina, and Sarah were more than happy to usher him outside and keep him busy with questions.

"At least someone has the right idea," Tara muttered irritably as she turned toward the men left behind. "You three. In the kitchen. Now."

She marched past them and didn't miss Mason's smart-mouthed, mocking comment, "Geez, bossy much?" Oh, he had no idea how *bossy* she was about to become.

Clay's kitchen was huge and spacious, completely renovated with state-of-the-art appliances and yards of counter space to cater to Samantha's love of baking. Evidence of her baking passion was set out on the counter—delicious cupcakes, fancy cookies, and decadent pastries. If Tara didn't have business to take care of, she would have beelined it straight to Samantha's desserts and indulged.

Once the four of them were all in the kitchen, she spun around to face them as they stood in a semicircle in front of her. "What the hell is going on with you three?" she asked, finally unleashing her frustration. "You're acting like complete jerks around Jackson and he doesn't deserve it."

"Learning about Jackson and the circumstances of his adoption hasn't been easy to digest," Clay said quietly as he moved toward the sink so he could look out the window to the deck and watch the girls and Jackson.

"And you think it's been a piece of cake for him?" She crossed her arms over her chest. "So you're going to punish him for something your drug-addicted mother did?"

"We're not trying to punish him," Levi said, shifting on his feet while Mason stood next to his brother with an obstinate frown on his face.

"It sure as hell feels that way." Her tone was haughty, and she didn't care. "You've ignored him since he came to the bar to meet you three last week."

Clay's gaze was riveted to whatever was going on outside, and he spoke over his shoulder. "We were going to contact him this week and see if he wanted to come by the bar and talk," he said, the slightest hint of guilt infusing his voice.

"Better late than never, I suppose," she said sarcastically. "Just keep in mind that there are three of you and *one* of him. You three have each other, but who does he have?"

"He has a *family*," Mason said abruptly. "That's what Jackson has. We three are the only family we've *ever* had, and it's not easy to let a virtual stranger in."

"That's the problem with the three of you." Her voice rose angrily as she encompassed all of them with a wild wave of her hand. "You have no idea what his life has been like, how he grew up and how he was treated and what kind of *family* he had. Are you judging him based on the suit he wore the first time he met you guys? Do you think that defines the man he is and somehow makes him impervious to a shitty childhood? Maybe he had it just as tough as you guys did."

Clay briefly looked away from the window, his gaze narrowed on Tara. "Why does it sound like you know all about his family and childhood?"

She ignored the slight accusation she heard in his voice. "Because maybe I've taken the time to talk to him. To get to know him. Something the three of you *should* have been doing."

"Jesus, you're so defensive," Mason muttered testily. "What's going on with you and him, anyway?"

Tara's heart suddenly beat a whole lot faster, because she knew what she was about to reveal was going to start another heated debate. "I should say that it's none of your damn business, but I have nothing to hide." She lifted her chin adamantly. "Jackson and I are dating."

"Dating?" Levi echoed, dumbfounded by her admission.

Whereas Mason was more vocal in his approach. "You're fucking *dating* him?" he asked incredulously.

"Jesus, Tara." Clay's lips flattened into a thin line of disapproval. "Why didn't you tell us?"

She stared at him as if he were an idiot. "Are you seriously asking me that question right now, after the shitty way you've acted toward Jackson?"

Clay glanced at both of his brothers, a silent message of concern passing between them—one they didn't seem willing to share with her. When Clay returned his attention to the women out on the deck with Jackson, a worrisome look straining his features, something inside of Tara detonated.

"Stop staring out the window like Jackson is some kind of mass murderer and you're worried he's going to slaughter your wife," she snapped heatedly.

Clay and Mason looked from her to Levi, that silent communication seemingly flowing between the three of them again.

She didn't like the uneasy vibe settling in the air. "What's going on?"

Levi scrubbed his hand along his jaw and expelled a deep breath, as if what he was about to tell her was difficult for him. "Tara, there's something you should know about Jackson. I know you're not going to be happy about this, but I had a friend run a background check on him, and he was charged with assault a few years back . . ."

She stiffened, feeling as though she'd been jolted with a live wire. Okay, she hadn't seen that coming. Granted, she and Jackson were in the beginning stages of getting to know one another, but physical violence and aggression didn't match up to the Jackson she knew.

"Assault for what?" she asked, giving in to her curiosity.

"The charge was dropped, so the reason isn't on record." Levi pushed his hands into the front pockets of his jeans, his gaze direct. "But the fact that he might have a temper concerns us."

Tara stared at Levi in disbelief. This from the brother who was the most sensible and levelheaded of the three. "For God's sake. Mason has a temper and nobody has shunned him! Have you forgotten that he was the one to beat the shit out of Sarah's ex?"

"You know what we mean, Tara," Clay said, trying to be rational.

No, she really *didn't* understand. She pursed her lips at Levi. "Did you find anything else on his record that might concern you?"

He hesitated a few seconds before answering. "No."

She arched a brow. "So it could be an isolated incident?"

"I suppose it could be."

"But you'd rather think the worst of him?" She looked at each brother and was somewhat gratified to see different degrees of guilt and contrition on their faces.

"We were just being cautious," Clay said gruffly.

"What happened to innocent until proven guilty?" Her voice grew softer as her anger ebbed away. "We all have a past, and we've all done things we're not proud of. I'm certainly not squeaky clean, and I would hate to think that any of you would judge me for being addicted to prescription drugs six years ago, or because someone I cared about died of an overdose when I was high myself."

She swallowed past the tight knot gathering in her

throat as she brought up that dark time in her life and the shame that came with it, but she had Clay's, Levi's, and Mason's attention, and that's what mattered to her. "You don't know the reasons surrounding the assault charge, so how about you give Jackson the benefit of the doubt until he gives you a reason to worry? If you knew what he'd been through in his life, you wouldn't judge him so harshly."

"You're right," Clay said quietly.

Levi nodded his agreement.

Mason begrudgingly gave her a look of acknowledgement.

"Just . . . be careful, okay?" Clay said, unable to completely let go of that protective trait he possessed when it came to the people in his life.

"I can take care of myself," she said with a smile. "I've been doing it a long time."

"Doesn't mean we can't worry about you," Levi said.

She'd said her piece and felt as though she could breathe easier now that she'd gotten everything off her chest. "Jackson is your brother. All he wants is to get to know you guys, so at least give him that chance without holding anything against him."

Clay gave her a sincere look. "Fair enough."

Tara was hopeful that she'd made headway with the brothers' stubborn mindset when it came to Jackson, but their cooperation remained to be seen.

JACKSON FOUND HIMSELF being entertained by three lively women while Tara was inside the house with Clay, Mason, and Levi—the women's vibrant personalities an antithesis to his brothers' more serious demeanors. Then again, he supposed that's why these ladies meshed so well with Clay, Mason, and Levi. It was a great example of opposites attract, strengths balancing weaknesses, and the philosophy behind all that yin-yang crap. With a dark, turbulent past like his brothers had gone through, these women no doubt provided a much-needed light and playful aspect to the relationships . . . just as Jackson realized Tara had done for him.

He leaned back against the deck railing, and as he took a bite of the most amazing cookie he'd ever tasted—a chocolate ganache French macaroon, according to Samantha—he listened to Katrina regale him with tales of Mason as an unruly teenager that made him laugh. His brother had been a defiant hellion and not much different from the man he detected even now. Jackson loved having insight to his brothers' past and hoped one day they'd be the ones to share these kinds of amusing stories with him. But for now, at least, he had three allies, and he'd take whatever he could get.

The topic of discussion shifted as Sara asked Jackson about being an architect, and at the same time, the sliding glass door leading onto the deck opened. Tara stepped out with a satisfied smile on her face, looking more relaxed and optimistic than when they'd first arrived. Clay, Mason, and Levi followed her, the wariness they'd initially greeted Jackson with now almost gone.

He had no idea what had transpired inside the house, but clearly Tara had worked some kind of magic. To the point that Jackson actually felt comfortable breaking the ice, so to speak, and initiating a casual conversation with Clay, who'd grabbed a bottle of beer from a vat of ice and came to stand next to his wife.

"You're a lucky man." Jackson's gaze met Clay's as he filched another macaroon from the tray on a nearby table. "Your wife is a phenomenal baker."

"Yeah, definitely one of the many qualities that won me over." Clay slid his arm around Samantha's waist to pull her close to his side. "But don't let this sweet, innocent face fool you. She's been known to bribe me for certain things with her desserts. Isn't that right, cupcake?" he asked affectionately.

"Bribe you?" Samantha refuted his claim with an amusing eye roll. "You're such a pushover, Saint Clay, whether you want to admit it or not."

Clay grinned at his wife, completely smitten, his adoration written all over his face.

"Oh, just wait until the baby is here," Katrina interjected enthusiastically. "I'm betting Daddy *and* the three uncles are going to be like giant marshmallows."

So easily, Katrina had included Jackson in that scenario, and he waited for one of his brothers to denounce his part in the baby's life, but much to his surprise, and profound relief, it never came.

Levi took a drink of the orange soda he'd retrieved from the cooler. "It'll be the first Kincaid baby, so of course we're going to spoil the hell out of the kid."

Mason smirked. "Even better that we can send that spoiled-rotten kid home for Clay to deal with."

Clay arched a dark brow at his brother. "You know, Mason, karma is a bitch. Just keep in mind what a hellion you were growing up and that what goes around, comes around, which means you're probably going to have a boy who breaks every fucking rule there is, and *I'll* be the one laughing my ass off."

Katrina gasped, her green eyes filled with feigned horror. "Oh, my God, if that's the case, I'm *never* getting pregnant."

Mason slung his arm around Katrina's neck and leaned toward her to whisper something private in her ear. Something lewd, judging by Katrina's appalled expression.

"I can't escape your *super sperm* so don't even try?" she repeated incredulously, then laughed at her husband's cocky statement, as did everyone else. "Are you serious right now?"

"One hundred percent serious." Mason waggled his brows at his wife, his gaze turning salacious as he nodded meaningfully toward the house. "Want to go test the theory?"

"Not in *my* goddamn bathroom," Clay barked out adamantly.

Again, everyone laughed, and Jackson knew he was

missing a key component in the conversation. A joke of some sort that everyone was privy to except him.

Tara must have seen the confusion on his face, because she linked her arm through his. The intimate gesture wasn't lost on him or anyone else standing there.

"Clay caught this now reformed man-whore in the ladies' bathroom at Kincaid's, with different women, on more than one occasion," she told Jackson.

"*Reformed* being the operative word." Mason nuzzled Katrina's neck and skimmed a hand possessively over her ass. "Now, my Kitty-Kat is the only woman I want, and all I can handle."

Katrina gave him a playful shove. "And don't you forget it."

Once the lighthearted teasing died down, Clay cleared his throat and glanced at Tara, a fond smile on his lips. "So, I'd like to be the first to formally say congratulations, Tara, on getting your business degree. You worked hard. You were dedicated. You juggled a late-night job, school during the day, and a whole lot of cramming for exams. It's a huge accomplishment we wanted to celebrate with you, and I couldn't be prouder that you finally did it."

She ducked her head in embarrassment, a warm, pink flush suffusing her cheeks. "Thank you. I seriously couldn't have done it without your support, Clay."

He shrugged off her gratitude. "You would have done it regardless, because that's who you are, Tara. A woman who is determined and committed to whatever she sets her mind to."

Everyone else echoed their agreement, telling Jackson just how much everyone cared about Tara and how much they meant to her in return. Tara had told him she didn't see her family very often, but shouldn't they have been at something as important as a party to celebrate their daughter's college degree?

He realized, for as much as Tara knew about him, he wanted—no, he *needed*—to know everything about her. Her secrets. Her pain. Her heartache and what made her the happiest. All those things mattered to him. *She* mattered to him.

Mason clapped his hands, getting everyone's attention. "Now that all the sappy sentiments are out of the way, let's get this party started!"

The women cheered in response, and the festivities were on. Over the next few hours, they grilled hamburgers, enjoyed the cake and desserts that Samantha had made, and Clay, Mason, and Levi made an effort to converse with Jackson. They asked where he went to college, where he currently lived, and about his job as an architect and what it entailed. They seemed genuinely interested, and while the topics were mostly superficial and nobody broached the subject of his family and childhood, it felt as though it was a start in the right direction.

After a while, Tara opened the presents that the girls had clearly bought for her, which included bath products, a gift card to her favorite boutique, and a narrow silver cuff bracelet that came in the well-known light blue box that signaled the gift was from Tiffany's. That last gift caused tears to fill Tara's eyes as she thanked everyone for being so thoughtful.

The day passed quickly, and to his surprise, Jackson enjoyed it immensely. Not only had his brothers warmed up but they seemed to relax around him as well, and that meant more to Jackson than anything. And he had Tara to thank.

The rapport was developing, the tension no longer a black cloud hanging over them, overshadowing their ability to truly get to know one another. Things weren't perfect, but their tentative acceptance felt like a solid start to something more.

And that was enough for Jackson. At least for now.

Chapter Eight

"**D**ID YOU HAVE a good time today?"

Jackson glanced at Tara, who was sitting in the passenger seat of his Porsche as he drove them back to her place. She looked good in his car, her stunning blue eyes bright with contentment and happiness and her long dark hair falling in soft, loose waves around her shoulders. The serene smile lifting the corners of her mouth made that sexy-as-hell diamond above her lip wink at him flirtatiously. He couldn't wait to kiss her again.

"I did have a nice time," he told her, which was true.

He'd enjoyed talking to the women and liked seeing the way they interacted with their significant others. Even his brothers, once they'd finally come out of the house with Tara, had been more open and seemed to relax with him as the afternoon and evening went on. Which made him curious to know what had transpired once Tara had ordered the three men into the kitchen while Jackson made his way outside with the girls.

"What did you say to the guys in the house that made them more amicable?" he asked.

Tara grinned at him. "In a nutshell, I told them to pull their heads out of their asses and be nice."

He chuckled as he shifted his gaze back to the road. "Well, it definitely worked."

"They're men. No sense in sugarcoating the truth," she said, a teasing lilt to her voice. "As we were leaving, I heard Clay ask you if you'd like to come by Kincaid's sometime next week to have a drink with him, Mason, and Levi."

Jackson hadn't expected the overture so soon, and he'd readily agreed since it was another opportunity to connect with his brothers. "Shocking, right?"

"No, not really. I think deep down inside, they really do want to get to know you better." She grew quiet and stared out the window, a pensive expression on her pretty face.

He reached across the console and squeezed her thigh. "Hey, where did you go?"

She turned her head and met his gaze, the soft blue lighting from the dashboard highlighting the hesitation he saw in the depths of her eyes. "I really want to ask you something, but I'll understand if it's something you don't want to talk about."

Okay, that was never a good sign, and while something pitched uneasily in his stomach, he had nothing to hide from her. "Sure. Go ahead and ask."

She worried on her lush lower lip for a second. "Levi mentioned that you were arrested for assault a few years ago but the charges were dropped. What happened?"

He swore beneath his breath and returned the hand that was on her leg to the steering wheel. "Is that why they've kept their distance? Because they thought I might be unstable?" And Jesus, they'd actually run a background check on him?

The quick flash of guilt that passed across her features was his answer, even though she didn't deny or confirm his question.

"I figured there was a good reason the charges were dismissed. I also pointed out to the guys that they don't have sterling pasts, either, and not to jump to conclusions they know nothing about."

"Thank you." The fact that she'd so staunchly defended him without knowing any of the facts of his arrest stirred something emotional in Jackson's chest. He wasn't used to anyone standing up for him. "If it was an issue, why didn't *they* just fucking ask me?"

"Because they're men, and therefore they're stubborn and hardheaded," she said as if that explained their actions.

He gave her a quick, sidelong glance at her description of the male population in general. "Just in case it's escaped your notice, *I'm* a man."

"Oh, yeah, I noticed. Quite a few times today." Her sweet, seductive voice stroked along his senses before she added more impartially, "And I'm sure you're not impervious to being obstinate about certain things yourself."

Okay, that was true. For the most part, men *were* stubborn creatures, and pride sometimes got in the way of rational thinking. He was definitely guilty of that a time or two over the years.

Reaching Tara's house, he pulled into the driveway and parked next to her compact car. He shut the engine off, and when she unbuckled her seat belt and moved to get out of the vehicle, he gently grabbed her arm to stop her.

She blinked at him questioningly.

"You wanted to know about the assault charge," he said, not wanting to bring this conversation into the house with them. Because once they stepped through the front door, there was only one thing he wanted between them . . . pure, unadulterated pleasure. And sinning. An entire night of it.

She shook her head. "Jackson . . . you don't have to tell me."

Without knowing *why* he'd been accused of a violent attack, she trusted him. The knowledge humbled him like nothing had in a very long time. He smiled and skimmed the backs of his fingers along her soft cheek, the caress tender and gentle. "If I tell you my secret, will you tell me one of yours?" he teased.

She stiffened ever so slightly. "What makes you think I have a secret to tell?"

That night at the donut shop, she'd been evasive

about a few things he figured were personal and private. "Don't we all?"

She swallowed hard, and he didn't miss the pained look in her gaze. "I don't want one secret to depend on the other. So if you don't want to share, I understand."

"You're right." Okay, maybe she wasn't ready to tell him what had put those shadows in her eyes, and he decided he was willing to wait until she was, of her own accord. "But I do want to tell you what happened to me."

She settled back into the leather seat and turned her body toward him. The street lamp in front of her house bathed the interior of the car in a soft glow of light, just enough for him to see the genuine kindness and caring etching her features.

"I was married a while ago," he started, and didn't miss the surprise that flickered in Tara's eyes at the admission. "Collette and I met at a work party and dated for about eight months before getting engaged. I honestly thought we had the same vision for our future, and we both talked about starting a family soon after we got married. I thought we were trying for a baby, that everything was great and wonderful, until I came home from work early one day and found her in our bed fucking a colleague. The guy was a cocky asshole. But he also had a shitload of family money that made me look like a pauper in comparison, and for Collette, that made his dick look a lot better than mine."

Tara quietly placed her hand over his, and he expelled a harsh breath.

"Was I angry to find her screwing another guy in our apartment? Hell, yes. But all I did was tell the prick to get the fuck out of my house, and he literally got in my face and shoved me, as if it was all somehow my fault. He was this short little shit with a Napoleon complex, and as soon as his hands touched me, my first instinct was to throw a punch to defend myself. That one and only blow shattered his perfect fucking nose and had blood streaming down his face." Jackson smirked in satisfaction.

Tara tried stifling a giggle behind her hand. "I know I shouldn't be laughing, but anyone stupid enough to pick a fight with you shouldn't be shocked when you flatten them. You're a big guy."

He shrugged. "It was just an instinctive reaction, and I didn't touch him after that, but the damage was done. Collette was screaming at me like I was a monster, and Brad called the cops to have me arrested for assault. A few weeks later, he dropped the charges because his family didn't want the publicity. I was grateful not to be dragged through a trial." He ran a hand through his hair. "I filed for divorce from Collette, and I can't say I was surprised when she married rich, trust-fund baby Brad as soon as the divorce papers were signed." He shrugged. "A short while after that, they had a kid, which was probably the hardest thing for me, since I believed that's where *my* marriage had been heading."

"I'm sorry," Tara said softly.

"It is what it is, right?" he said, and they both smiled.

He shook his head. "You know, I feel like most of my life has been a series of blindsides. Just when I feel complacent or comfortable, something comes along to shatter that illusion."

She tipped her head to the side. "Like what?"

Where did he start? The list was a long one. "Being an only child and my mother doting on me until my brother, Oliver, was born and that all changed without me understanding why. Getting married only to have my ex-wife cheat on me with someone with a bigger, more attractive bank account than I had. Finding out I was adopted and had a twin and other siblings I knew nothing about and having to prove myself to them. It seems like whenever I feel good about my life in general, something else happens to shake everything up all over again."

She leaned over the console and surprised him by placing a warm, endearing kiss on his lips. "It's a good thing you're resilient," she murmured affectionately as she started to move away.

Those generous words stirred something in him, and he slid his hand around the back of her neck, drawing her mouth right back to his for a hot, deep, hungry kiss that conveyed his desire for her and the feelings of undeniable need she evoked whenever he was with her. As their tongues chased and entwined and she moaned against his lips, Jackson realized that *she* was that good thing in his life, and damned if he didn't want to hold tight to her and protect what was growing between them so it didn't get taken away, too.

Eventually, he ended the kiss. Her lashes fluttered open and she smiled at him like a vixen. "So . . . are you coming inside?"

He grinned wickedly at the unintended double entendre. "Care to elaborate where?"

Her laugh was both husky and naughty as she nipped playfully at his bottom lip. "Coming inside the house . . . coming inside me . . ."

His dick swelled beneath the zipper of his jeans. "Fuck yeah. To both."

"Then let's go." She moved back to her side of the car, opened the door, and sent him a coquettish look over her shoulder. "If I remember correctly, you promised me many different ways to sin."

He groaned and quickly retrieved the strip of condoms he'd put into the glove compartment earlier to make sure he was prepared so they didn't get to the point of no return only to realize neither one of them had any protection. He stuffed them into the front pocket of his jeans, got out of the vehicle and set the alarm, then grabbed her hand as they walked up to the door. Once they were inside the house, she switched on one of the lamps in the living room and set her purse down on the couch.

Suddenly, she looked nervous and unsure, very unlike the confident woman he knew her to be—and even had been a few minutes ago. He had no idea what to make of her unexpected anxiety or what had prompted it.

"Is everything okay?" he asked.

She twisted her fingers in front of her and wouldn't meet his gaze. "Before we do this, there's something I need to tell you."

Concerned, he closed the short distance between them and gently grabbed her hands, pulling them apart and forcing her to look up at him. "What's going on, Tara? Are you having second thoughts about us tonight?" He hated to think that was a possibility, but he'd respect any decision she made.

"No . . ." She shook her head, causing her silky hair to swirl around her shoulders. "It's just that . . . I haven't had sex in six years." Her cheeks flushed with embarrassment.

Her confession momentarily rendered him speechless, but it certainly wasn't any kind of deal breaker for him. "That's a long time," he said, rubbing his thumbs along the pulse point in her wrists. "Is there a specific reason?"

Her shoulder lifted in a bashful shrug. "Honestly, there hasn't been anyone I've wanted to be with . . . until you."

His breath left his lungs as he stared at her in stunned disbelief. *Fucking hell.* She was so beautiful, so sexy and goddamn tempting, it was hard to imagine that in six years no other man had had the pleasure of fucking this gorgeous woman. That she hadn't been attracted to any other man enough to give her body over to one. Until now. With him.

She shifted uncertainly on her feet. "I just wanted you to know, in case things are . . . awkward at first."

Remembering how she'd responded to him when he'd kissed her outside of the donut shop, how she'd nearly spontaneously combusted in his arms, there was no worry that anything about tonight would be even remotely uncomfortable. "Six years is a hell of a long time to be celibate," he said, humor suffusing his voice. "Are you sure you're ready to break that dry spell?"

"I'm sure, unless you're suddenly having performance anxiety?" She raised a sassy brow, provoking him just as brazenly, back to the self-assured woman he enjoyed.

He chuckled. Oh, yeah, they were going to be just fine.

"Fucking tease," he said on a low, sexual growl. "I'll show you a performance."

Gripping her waist, he took a few steps forward, at the same time guiding her backward, until her shoulders were pressed against the nearest vertical surface. He slipped his hands beneath the hem of her blouse and pushed the fabric up her torso and over her breasts. She automatically lifted her arms as he pulled the top over her head and dropped it to the floor. He reached around to unclasp her bra and added that lacy piece of lingerie to the pile next to her feet. He took a moment to look his fill of her gorgeous tits, round and full and perfectly shaped, watched for a few more seconds in avid appreciation how they trembled with each ragged breath she took.

Her anticipation was palpable, and he finally gave in to temptation, filling both of his hands with her soft, lush breasts and plucking her already stiff nipples with his fingers.

She moaned deep in her throat, her eyes glazing over with lust. "Jackson . . . my room is down the hall."

"Right here is fine for now," he murmured huskily as he lowered his mouth and kissed the side of her throat. "If I get you anywhere near a bed, I'm going to fucking lose control. There are way too many things I want to do to you before I have you spread out on a mattress for me to enjoy."

She pushed her fingers into his hair, clutching the strands tight in her fists. He traced his tongue along her neck and felt the goose bumps rising on her skin and puckering the velvet-soft flesh of her areolas.

He smiled against her ear as he lightly skimmed his fingers down her stomach to the waistband of her jeans. "Just lean back against the wall and let me get you ready for my cock. I want your pussy nice and wet and slick, so a few orgasms before I fuck you ought to do the trick."

Her breathing hitched, and already he felt her melting, her body yielding to his seduction just like he wanted. He unsnapped her jeans and lowered the zipper, letting his fingers graze over the silky fabric covering her mound in a lazy, promising caress.

She made an impatient sound in the back of her throat and pushed her hips against his hand. "Jackson . . . *please.*"

He lifted his head so he could look at her face, her full lips parted and damp from the sweep of her tongue. Her cheeks were flushed with desire, her eyes dark and delirious with need. A need he was solely responsible for, and that arousing knowledge made him harder than fucking granite.

Ignoring the insistent throb of his dick, he continued to slide his hand into her panties, watching the rapturous expression on her face as he glided two long fingers along her damp sex and lightly tweaked her swollen clit. She gasped and attempted to rock against his touch, brazenly trying to control the pressure and friction she needed to climax.

"Not yet, greedy girl," he said, refusing to allow her to top him from the bottom. He wanted to be the one to give her every orgasm she had tonight. Wanted each and every one to be so fucking intense she'd crave more of him.

"Put your hands on your breasts," he ordered in a low, deep voice. "Lift them to my mouth so I can suck on your nipples while my fingers fuck your pussy."

She was quick to follow his command, pushing her tits up to his parted lips, presenting them like the offering they were. He licked across one pebbled tip, then the other, before drawing one deep into his mouth. Between her legs, he stroked her soft, wet flesh, his fingers mimicking the dip and swirl of his tongue on her breast.

Her head fell back against the wall, her entire body shuddering from the dual assault. She moved shamelessly against his palm, her hips instinctively thrusting, and this time he let her fuck his hand, let her ride his fingers as he pushed two deep inside her tight, slick core and rubbed the tips against that sensitive spot that made a soft cry escape her lips.

Knowing she was about to come, he lifted his head from her breasts with one last scrape of his teeth to her nipples, wanting to watch her expression as she climaxed. Wanting her to see him and know that he was the one making her fly apart.

"Look at me, Tara," he commanded gruffly.

Her lashes fluttered open, her soft, hazy blue eyes meeting his desperately. Without words, she was begging him to give her the release her body was clamoring for. Another deep plunge of his fingers, another rhythmic caress of his thumb against that sweet spot between her legs, and she whimpered as she started to unravel from the inside out.

Her breathing grew erratic. Frantic hands gripped his shoulders for something to hold on to as her inner walls clenched around the fingers buried deep inside of her, and a flood of arousal coated his hand. She shuddered, her hips jerking hard as sensation battered her body, and the fucking icing on the cake was when Tara screamed his name, letting him know she was completely aware of exactly who'd taken her over that edge.

She'd been worried that this first time would be awkward, and he was pretty fucking sure he'd dispelled that concern. In fact, he couldn't remember seeing anything as stunning as Tara in the throes of ecstasy, and he couldn't wait to take her there again.

When she finally came back to the present, he removed his hand from her jeans, and he made sure she was watching when he brought his wet fingers to his lips and sucked two of them into his mouth. Her eyes widened in shock, and he gave her a wicked grin as he slowly pulled them back out with a low, delectable sound of pleasure.

"Fuck, you taste good," he said on a blissful groan. "Hot and sweet, like goddamn honey. I can't wait to lap all that sugar up with my tongue."

Even in the dim lighting from the one lamp she'd turned on in the living room, there was no mistaking the self-conscious way she bit her bottom lip and wouldn't meet his gaze. Clearly, she wasn't used to such explicit dirty talk or even filthier sexual games. Then again, she had six years of catching up to do, and he was guessing any lovers she'd had prior to him had never been so frank about what, exactly, they wanted to do to her.

He didn't have that problem. He was going to have all the fun of stripping away her inhibitions, all the satisfaction of corrupting her. Lucky him.

First things first, he touched her jaw and made her look at him. "Don't go getting all shy on me now, sweetheart. That was just orgasm number one. We still have a whole lot of sinning left to do."

"I'm not being shy. I've just never had a guy . . . do that before."

"What, lick the delicious taste of your pussy from his fingers?" He chuckled, because she looked adorable when she was flustered, and he couldn't resist teasing her. "It's no different than me going down on you with my mouth, which fucking sounds like a great idea to me right now."

Before she could say another word—because he was done wasting time talking when they had better, hotter, more pleasurable things to do—he swept her up into his arms, dismissing her gasp of surprise as he headed in the direction she'd indicated earlier. Ignoring the way her bare breasts bounced with each step he took required much more effort.

"Which room?" he asked, seeing a few doors to his right and left.

"The one at the very end on the right."

He walked inside and set her on her feet by the end of the bed. The adjoining bathroom was a few steps away, and he walked over and turned on the light so there was just enough illumination for him to see her alluring body and her breathtaking curves as he came back to her again.

He toed off his shoes and removed his socks. Her jeans were still unbuttoned and unzipped, and he grabbed the waistband of her pants and slowly pushed the denim material and her silky panties over her hips and down to her thighs, then helped her out of the tangle of clothing. She stood in front of him, completely naked, with a vulnerable glimmer in her eyes that told him this wasn't just any ordinary fuck for her.

It wasn't for him, either. There hadn't been anything ordinary about her, or the feelings she evoked in him, since the first moment they'd met.

"Sit down on the edge of the bed," he murmured.

She complied, keeping her legs demurely together, which he'd allow for now, though that momentary show of modesty did make him smile as he pulled his shirt over his head and dropped it to the floor. It was as though she was struggling with two distinct versions of herself—a sweet good girl who didn't want to appear too overtly eager and a wanton dirty girl who wanted to indulge in provocative, steamy fantasies. Tonight, he was going to coax the uninhibited bad girl to come out to play.

He reached into the front pocket of his jeans and withdrew the half dozen rubbers he'd brought with him and tossed them onto the bed next to her. She glanced at the foil wrappers, then back up at him with an impressed smile on her lips.

"That's a lot of condoms," she said, one of her dark brows rising inquisitively. "Feeling extra lucky tonight?"

He smirked. "Oh, you have no idea just how lucky I'm feeling."

When he slowly began opening the front of his jeans, her gaze dropped to where his hands were, and yeah, he was fucking gratified to hear the hitch of anticipation that tangled in her throat as she caught sight of the thick bulge straining against the boxer briefs he wore. He stripped the rest of his clothes off and straightened, and that uneven inhale of breath he'd just heard turned into a low, strangled moan as she stared unabashedly at his sizeable erection.

Her jaw dropped open slightly, and she absently licked her lips, as if she were already tasting him on her tongue, in her mouth. The hungry look in her eyes had his dick jerking in response.

"Stop looking at my cock like that, or you'll be on your knees with it halfway down your throat within the next thirty seconds," he warned, almost not recognizing the harsh, dominant sound of his own voice.

She blinked up at him, her hands clutching the comforter on the bed as sublime lust played across her features. "I don't think I'd mind that at all."

Jesus. Fucking. Christ. His dick was totally on board with that idea, and he had to seriously remind himself that tonight was all about Tara and not watching her lips slide up and down his shaft as she sucked him off. "I'm going to hold you to that promise, another time. Right now, I want you to spread those gorgeous legs for me. Show me that sweet pussy I'm dying to taste again."

She did as he'd ordered, and he knelt in front of her, his gaze devouring all that erotically smooth skin, the soft lips of her pussy, the pretty pink petals of her sex. He glanced a little higher and saw a tattoo on the lower left side of her bikini line. It was all script and read: *The struggle is part of the story.*

There was so much emotion and meaning behind those words, and while he was curious to know the significance of the ink, he saved the question for later. Right now this was part of *their* story, and he wanted his first time with her to exceed her expectations and leave her completely sated.

"Lie back and close your eyes," he instructed as he pressed his hands to her knees to open her even wider. "I'm going to make you feel so fucking good."

Chapter Nine

TARA WAS A slave to Jackson's every command. Whatever he asked, she obeyed without question, wanting to experience every single level of intimate pleasure with this man. She'd never felt so worshipped, so beautiful and desirable as she did with him.

She lay back and closed her eyes as he'd requested, and once she was supine, he lowered his head and placed a warm, openmouthed kiss on the inside of one of her thighs, then used his teeth and tongue to inflame her even more. Leisurely, he made his way up one quivering leg, then did the same to the other, and there was no holding back her desperate, needy moans as he finally reached the place she was dying to feel his mouth the most.

He draped both her limbs over his broad shoulders and slid his hands up to grip her hips, then moved in closer, the warm gust of his breath against her exposed flesh shooting tingles up her spine. The tip of his tongue teased through her folds, tantalizing her with the lightest of touches, and she made a sound of frustration that did nothing to speed up his torment. He took his time, learning what made her sigh, what made her moan, and ultimately, what made her whimper and writhe beneath the onslaught of his incredibly talented mouth.

"Jackson," she whispered desperately as desire coiled tight in her belly and the ache he'd created between her legs swelled hotter and higher inside of her. Beyond any semblance of modesty, she fisted her fingers into his hair and lifted her hips toward his mouth, seeking . . . *more*.

With a low, ragged groan, he finally obliged, the slow, lazy licks along her slit increasing into firmer, deeper strokes that had her panting, a wild need racing through her body. His ravenous lips slid across every inch of her pussy and sucked on her sensitive clit, devouring her as if she were the sweetest dessert imaginable. His mouth was hot and wet, his tongue relentless in its quest to send her over the edge and straight into ecstasy.

She was nearly there. Her orgasm swelled to epic proportions inside of her, and she arched her back, twisting her fingers tighter in his hair as she shamelessly, brazenly, bucked against his depraved, proficient mouth. Her trembling thighs tightened against the sides of his head, the chafing of his stubble on her tender skin amplifying all the other arousing sensations battering her. The light, erotic scrape of his teeth across her clit and a deep thrust of his tongue had a monumental climax slamming into her so hard she cried out as wave after wave of the most intense pleasure consumed her, physically and emotionally.

She collapsed back onto the mattress and released his hair from her fingers. As her body pulsed with the delicious aftershocks of such a fierce orgasm and her gasps slowly ebbed into sated sighs, Tara was vaguely aware of Jackson standing and reaching for one of the condoms he'd tossed onto the bed next to her.

Through heavy eyelids that she could only manage to open half-mast considering what a limp, boneless heap she was, she blatantly ogled his naked body. He was gorgeous—lightly muscled, with defined abs, lean hips, and . . . Jesus, he was well endowed. Thick, with way more length and girth than her battery-operated boyfriend, that was for sure.

He glanced up at her as he sheathed his engorged dick, catching her sudden wide-eyed stare. A cocky smile eased up the corners of the sinful mouth that had just given her such unparalleled bliss. "Don't worry," he teased with a devilish twinkle in his dark eyes as he stroked his shaft in his hand. "You're so wet and slick it'll fit just fine."

She laughed softly, even as her body responded to the way his fingers tugged on his erection. "Arrogant much?"

"Nothing egotistical about the truth," he said, his gaze dropping to where her legs were still splayed open. Where her sex was glistening from the orgasm he'd just given her. "In a minute, when I'm buried balls deep inside your soft, wet pussy and you're stretched tight around me, I'm sure you'll agree."

She licked her lips at the thought of taking all of him and realized she was way more excited than nervous. "Six years," she reminded him as she started to move up the bed to make room for him. "Go easy on me."

"You're not going anywhere." With a wicked grin, he grabbed her ankles and pulled her back down to the foot of the bed so that her ass was right on the edge again. "I'm going to fuck you right here, just like this, so I can watch you take every inch of my cock."

His big hands slid down her calves to the backs of her knees, his fingers gripping there as he widened her legs, then bent them toward her stomach. The unobstructed view he had of her sex, from her unveiled clit all the way down to her opening, was shocking and indecent. The hold he had on her was assertive and commanding, making it difficult for her to move, even if she wanted to.

Adrenaline rushed through Tara, and she instinctively grabbed on to the comforter for some kind of anchor. God, she'd never felt so sexually vulnerable. So exposed. So undeniably excited as she waited for him to take her in such a dominant way. There was nothing conventional about this man when it came to sex, but that's what made him so hot. So sexy. So thrilling.

He let go of one of her knees, just long enough to

drag the tip of his cock through all the moisture he'd just enticed from her, then aligned the head at the entrance of her body. His hand returned to her leg, repositioning it wide open so he could still see everything as he pushed his hips forward, and his cock demanded entrance. She moaned at the initial pressure, inhaled a sharp breath as he breached her tight channel, and was purring with pleasure by the time his shaft was seated completely inside her.

She'd never felt so indulgently, wonderfully full. "You fit me more than just fine," she said, compelled to give credit where it was due.

"Told you so," he murmured seductively, arrogantly, as he leisurely withdrew, then gradually impaled her on his cock again, his eyes never leaving the place where they were joined.

He slow-fucked her, sliding all the way in with a deliberate grind of his hips, then pulling almost all the way back out, drawing out every intimate sensation her pliant body had to offer. It was pure torment and the most exquisite temptation. Every sleek stroke of his cock along her inner walls was an erotic massage and a completely maddening tease, and all she could do was moan and let him have his way with her.

"Touch yourself, Tara," he ordered gruffly. "I want to watch you make yourself come while I fuck you. I want to feel your orgasm squeezing my cock as I come."

She shivered at Jackson's dark demeanor. God, he was stripping her of every single inhibition she had. All in one night. And a part of her wanted to see that control of his break, too. Wanted to be the one to push him over that edge and make him wild with desire. To the point that he was frantic and took her as hard and deep as he wanted. As he needed.

Doing as he asked, she smoothed her flattened palm down her stomach toward her pussy. Her nipples tightened to aching points as he continued to pump unhurriedly in and out of her, his heated gaze tracking the movement of her hand as it reached her mound and she glided her fingers between her soft, swollen lips, through the hot, wet moisture coating her sex. A little lower, and the tips of her fingers grazed the length of his cock as he pulled out of her, and with a low, primitive sound erupting in the back of his throat, his hips jerked a little harder against her.

His jaw clenched in restraint as his hands gripped her legs tighter to keep her pinned to the bed, his breathing slightly erratic. Tara hid a secret smile. She liked that her touch had an effect on him, that it threatened his taut discipline. Seeing that slip in his composure bolstered her confidence, made her feel daring and seductive.

With his eyes glued between her thighs, she toyed with her clit, still sensitive from her recent climax. But it felt good, too, especially when coupled with Jackson's shaft tunneling deep inside of her. She rubbed in small circles, her fingers sweeping over that sweet spot more and more rapidly as the promise of another orgasm beckoned.

Without thinking, she lifted her free hand to one of her breasts, squeezing the soft mound of flesh and giving her nipple the kind of pinch that caused a chain reaction of pleasure from her chest all the way down to where their bodies became one. As she moaned and squeezed her inner muscles around his cock, his breathing grew harsh, the lust dilating his eyes fanning the flames igniting deep inside her.

His fingers gripped her legs so tightly Tara was certain he'd leave marks of his possession. "Jesus . . ." His voice came out on a low, feral growl as his hips began to move faster, his shaft driving deeper, his control suddenly unraveling at an accelerated pace. "I'm going to fucking come . . . so . . . goddamn . . . *hard.*"

She gasped as each of his unbridled thrusts propelled her higher, pushing her to limits she'd never reached before. "Me, too," she whispered raggedly, her fingers finding that perfect rhythm against her clit.

"Do it," he said through gritted teeth as he continued to fill her with relentless need. "Do it fucking *now.*"

As if her body was his to master, Tara surrendered to the release crashing through her. She cried out incoherently as she convulsed around his hard flesh, as she felt his cock pulse with his own searing climax. Head thrown back, he groaned and shuddered and slammed to the hilt inside of her—stealing her breath, claiming her body, and owning a piece of her soul.

JACKSON AWOKE TO the most beautiful sight imaginable early the next morning. One he knew he could easily get used to. He was a side sleeper, and apparently so was Tara, because at some point during the night—after he'd fucked her a half dozen different ways—they'd ended up lying on her bed facing one another, their heads on individual pillows, their bodies less than a foot apart.

He smiled as he took in the view of Tara's soft, delicate features as she slept, enjoying how peaceful and content she looked and loving the fact that he was responsible for that sated flush still tingeing her cheeks. Her dark hair spilled across her white pillow, her black eyelashes stood out as they swept across her creamy complexion, and her full lips were slightly parted, reminding him that there was one thing they hadn't indulged in last night, and that was him feeling her warm, eager mouth sucking his cock.

The morning wood he'd woken up with throbbed at the erotic images filling his head. His unruly dick was acting as though it hadn't been deep inside Tara's pussy six times last night. Then again, Jackson was quickly coming to realize that he couldn't get enough of her, didn't want to, actually. And considering her avid reaction to every new sexual position he'd introduced her to, he was pretty damn sure the feeling was mutual.

He'd discovered that Tara's body was like a flower, blooming after a long winter's respite. With each touch and his unfiltered, explicit words, he'd awakened her desires, roused her passions, and it was so fucking hot to watch Tara give herself over to all the carnal pleasures he'd coaxed—and sometimes demanded—from her gorgeous, responsive body.

She sighed softly in her sleep, and even that small sound had the ability to turn him on. The sheet was pulled up to her chest, and he had to seriously resist the urge to caress his fingers along her bare arm, to gently push her to her back, pull down the covers, and suck on her nipples until he had her writhing beneath him and begging for his cock.

He was so damn tempted, but he'd exhausted her last night, and she probably needed a break. So he decided to take a shower, then make her breakfast. But once she had food in her stomach, all bets were off, he thought with a smirk.

He moved off the bed without waking her and strolled naked into the adjoining bathroom, quietly closing the door. He turned on the shower to let the water get hot. As he waited, he saw toothpaste on the vanity, and since he didn't have a toothbrush, he did the next best thing and washed his hands, then used his finger until his breath tasted minty fresh.

Stepping into the glass enclosure, he doused his entire body, then glanced at the array of feminine products on a rack in front of him. He had a choice between floral-smelling shampoo and fruity-scented body wash. Nothing even remotely masculine, but with limited options, he went for the peach shower gel.

He drizzled the thick liquid onto a pink mesh body scrubber and got the job done. He even used it to wash his hair. He rinsed off, using his palms to wick away the soap suds on his arms, his chest, and down his stomach. A frustrated groan escaped him as his fingers brushed across his stiff, aching erection. Fuck. He was never going to get through the morning with a persistent bulge in his pants if he didn't give his cock what it wanted.

"You're such a demanding fucker," he muttered irritably to himself as he leaned his back against the tiled wall and wrapped his fingers tight around his length. He closed his eyes to summon any one of the fantasies he'd created with Tara last night as he started to jack off.

After experiencing Tara in the flesh, his dick was "*meh*" about getting a hand job, and not the least bit impressed with his efforts. Jesus. Not only a demanding fucker but now he was becoming a selective asshole, as well. Jackson dropped his head back and utilized all his normal tricks to get the job done. His shaft remained hard as steel and mocked his attempts to get him off. He swore beneath his breath and pumped harder, faster . . .

"Want some help with that?"

Jackson jumped at the sound of Tara's soft, seductive voice. He'd been concentrating so hard he hadn't heard her enter the bathroom and had no idea how long she'd been standing on the other side of the glass partition, watching him. Judging by the amusement

fucking. Her body felt more vital and alive than it had since that incredibly dark time in her life. It was merely a bonus that Jackson also made her feel beautiful, desirable, and happy.

After getting out of the shower, she dressed in a pair of soft cotton shorts and a tank top—sans a bra for now—and used her blow dryer to remove most of the moisture from her hair so that it was damp but would dry in soft waves. She brushed her teeth, then followed the scent of something enticing and savory, along with the smell of coffee, to the kitchen.

Jackson was standing at her stove cooking breakfast, his back to her. His hair was still wet from his shower and looked as though he'd already run his fingers through it a few times. He was wearing only his jeans, giving her a spectacular view of his broad shoulders and his smooth, lightly muscled back and the tight ass encased in denim. Quietly, she padded across the tiled floor in her bare feet, and when she was standing behind him, she skimmed her fingers down his spine to the waistband of his jeans.

He glanced over his shoulder at her, a sexy smile on his lips. "Hey, beautiful. You hungry?"

"Umm, very." She wrapped her arms around his waist, flattened her hands on his firm stomach, and placed a soft, warm kiss on his back. She inhaled the scent of her body wash lingering on his skin and grinned. "Maybe I'll just take a big bite out of you. You smell like a delicious, juicy peach."

He chuckled, the sound wicked. "You can eat me,

lick me, and suck me later. I promise. Right now, I think we both need *real* food."

She couldn't disagree. She was starved. "And caffeine," she added, gravitating toward the coffeemaker. "I didn't get much sleep last night since a certain someone kept me up for hours."

"If you're expecting an apology, it's not gonna happen," he replied unrepentantly as he flipped a monstrous omelet in the large pan he had on the stove. "Not once in the *six times* that I fucked you did I hear that mouth of yours say, 'I'm tired, let me sleep.' So really, it's your own fault."

She laughed as she stirred cream and sugar into her coffee, then moved to the counter next to the stove and leaned against it. "I have to admit, your stamina is impressive."

Turning off the burner, he plated the fluffy egg dish, set it on the counter beside her hip, then kissed her mouth as he murmured, "My dick was totally influenced by the softest, warmest, tightest pussy it's ever had. *Yours.*"

She bit her bottom lip as a heated flush swept across her freshly scrubbed cheeks. She shouldn't be embarrassed after all the delightfully depraved things he'd done to her last night, but Jesus, the man had the dirtiest, filthiest mouth and had a way of catching her off guard with his shocking statements.

He took the coffee mug from her hands and set it aside, then grabbed her waist and lifted her until she was sitting on the counter. She gasped in startled surprise as he pushed her knees apart and moved in between so that her legs bracketed his hips.

"What are you doing?" she asked breathlessly.

He gave the mug back to her to hold and shrugged. "You only had enough eggs in the refrigerator for one omelet, so we're going to have to share."

She'd had at least a half carton of eggs, so his idea of what constituted *one* omelet was a huge serving size, not to mention the ham, mushrooms, and cheese he'd overstuffed it with. "I do have a table we can sit at, you know."

"Yeah, I know," he said, his eyes bright with amusement as he brought a forkful of eggs to her mouth. "But this is much more convenient. And fun."

"You're going to feed me my breakfast?" she asked incredulously.

A bad-boy grin lifted the corners of his lips. "It's the least I can do to thank you for that phenomenal blow job you just gave me. So just relax and enjoy, okay?

She rolled her eyes. "Okay. Fine."

She took the bite he offered and had to admit that he made one amazingly good omelet. For every one bite he fed to her, he ate two, not that she minded since he probably needed the calories more than she did. And once she *did* relax, she realized how much she appreciated being the center of his attention. She felt spoiled and pampered and cared for . . . and those were luxuries she'd lived most of her life without.

She just needed to be careful and not get too used

to Jackson's sole focus and attention. Whatever this was between them, it was amazing and exciting, but she knew better than to read more into this affair than what it currently was. There was no telling how long it would last, and it had taken her once broken, damaged heart so long to heal that she was cautious about giving someone that part of herself again.

They finished the breakfast he'd made, and Jackson rinsed the plate off, then came back to where she was still sitting on the counter. She expected him to help her down, but instead he braced his hands on either side of her thighs, his expression suddenly more serious than it had been since leaving Clay's the night before.

He exhaled a deep breath, his eyes so gentle it made her heart ache because she couldn't remember the last time anyone had looked at her with such understanding and affection. "So, now that you have a full stomach, there's something I'd like to ask you, but I'll understand if it's something you don't want to talk about."

She swallowed hard, feeling uneasy. Those were pretty much the same words she'd spoken to him last night, before she'd asked about his assault charge. When he'd turned around and asked her about *her* secrets and she'd managed to evade the question.

"Okay," she replied, hating the slight quiver in her voice and the dread of the unknown question coming her way.

"I saw your tattoo last night," he said, his gaze

holding hers steadily. "What does 'The struggle is part of the story' mean?"

An involuntary shiver stole through her, and her heart started a slow pound in her chest, increasing the anxiety quickening her pulse. The significance of the phrase she'd had Mason tattoo on her was personal and private, and no one had seen it until Jackson. It was a reminder of the journey she'd started over six years ago and the grief and anguish she'd survived. But was she ready to crack open a sealed part of her heart and share those painful memories with this man?

He slowly lifted a hand, and with excruciating gentleness, he brushed the backs of his fingers along her cheek in a soothing caress. "Sweetheart, whatever just put that panic I can clearly see in your eyes, whatever it is, it can't be that bad."

He was wrong. It *was* that bad. She inhaled a shaky breath, torn between pushing him away so she could put distance between them and being brave and sharing her biggest, most devastating secret with him. Part of her fear was that he'd look at her differently, that he'd see her more as an ex-drug addict who had no place in his successful life than a woman still trying to find her place in the world.

He was waiting patiently, not pushing or prodding for answers, leaving the end result totally up to her. She'd only known Jackson a short time, but there was one thing she knew without question—he was a man of integrity, one who valued honesty and trust, both of which he'd given to *her*. If he could allow her insight into his past, to the shitty childhood he'd endured and the betrayal of his ex-wife, couldn't she do the same?

The initial dread and fear she'd experienced slowly faded away as Jackson gave her as much time as she needed to make her decision. Letting anyone close was difficult for Tara when she was so used to protecting her emotions. Allowing someone to witness her greatest failure, to learn about the stupid choices she'd made that had led to a dark depression of guilt that had nearly swallowed her whole was even more challenging.

But maybe this moment with Jackson, this particular emotional struggle, was also a part of the story—and with that realization, she knew she had two choices. She could let the past continue to keep her from truly being whole and at peace with herself, or she could release the pain and take a step toward her future and the possibility of finding something special and unique with this man.

When presented that way, her decision became an easy one.

The calm that suddenly settled over Tara was exactly what she needed to know that she'd come to the right conclusion. "I think for you to truly understand the entire story, I need to tell you how I grew up."

He set his hands on her knees, not in a sexual way but as a reassurance that he was right there with her. "Okay."

"Do you remember me telling you that my father is an army sergeant at Camp Butler in Springfield?"

When he nodded, she continued. "Well, growing up with a parent in the military was tough. When I was really young, he was stationed overseas, so I only saw him a few times a year, but around the time I turned eight, he accepted a position at a base close to home, and the dynamic of our family completely changed. I always knew he was strict, because that's how he treated me and my brother when he was home on leave, but having him living with us full-time, well . . . it was bad."

Jackson didn't say a word, but then he didn't have to. The compassion in his eyes reached out to her, and the calming sensation of his thumb gently stroking her skin right above her knee was exactly the connection to him that she needed.

"My father was very hard-edged and stern, and he had certain expectations of me and my brother that seemed, at times, impossible to live up to. Nothing we did was good enough, ever." She shook her head as she remembered how beaten down and inadequate she'd felt, how her self-esteem had gradually dwindled along with what little she'd had left of her pride. "Anything below an A in school was unacceptable and we were punished. The chores we were expected to do around the house were endless, but the fact that he found fault in everything I did was what made life with him so excruciating. There was never any positive reinforcement, no praise for a job well done, because in his mind, my brother and I could do better, be better."

"What about your mother?" he asked quietly.

"My mother was passive and timid and would never contradict anything my father said or did. Even if she knew he was wrong or out of line, she never stood up to him, and that made me so fucking angry as a teenager. Especially when, as I got older, my father would criticize the clothes I wore, the style of my hair, the friends I had . . . and she never, not once, said a goddamn word in my defense."

Tara's throat tightened as memories of how hurt and betrayed she'd felt toward her mother during that time resurfaced now. "My mother's inability to get a backbone so she could protect me and my brother from our father's mental and emotional abuse only fueled my rage toward the entire situation. By the time I was sixteen, I was deliberately breaking every fucking rule my father made because it didn't make any difference if I followed them or not, because I couldn't do anything right, anyway. By the time I was eighteen, I was running with a bad crowd and abusing prescription drugs because it was the only thing that numbed my emotions and made my life bearable."

Jackson swore beneath his breath, and he picked up her hands, his fingers so warm compared to how cold she felt. He held her hands as if he wanted her to know that he was right there with her, listening to every word and empathizing with her family situation considering what he'd gone through with the man who'd raised him. Except her circumstance, and the choices she'd made, had led to a tragic ending she'd been too naive to ever see coming.

She forced herself to continue. "By the time I was nineteen, my father had kicked me out of the house because, according to him, I was a disgrace, and he wasn't going to support a drug addict in any way. Never once did he or my mom try and get me the help I desperately needed to get clean and sober, so I spent the next few years crashing on friends' couches and doing whatever it took to get ahold of oxycodone so I didn't have to feel anything . . . and that's how I met Michael."

"Michael?" he prompted curiously.

She nodded, trying to maintain her composure as she finished her story, but it was difficult considering what she was about to relive. "Michael, a guy I ended up getting involved with, was from a wealthy family, and he had emotional issues of his own that opiates helped him escape. We were together for a few months, and he had some connections to a dealer who sold the street version of fentanyl, which is one of the strongest painkillers on the market. We didn't know at the time, but the fentanyl was laced with heroin, and we both overdosed."

Her voice cracked, and she could feel the swell of moisture burning in her eyes. "Our roommate at the time found both of us unconscious the following morning, and we were taken to the hospital. I survived, but Michael . . . died." Hot, scalding tears fell over her lashes and tracked down her cheeks. "His family, when they came to the hospital, blamed me for his death. His sister, Brynn, said the most horrible, hateful things to me, and I just wanted to die from the pain I'd caused her family, even though it wasn't directly my fault. I've never felt such loathing and contempt from a person."

"Jesus, I'm so sorry." He raised both of his hands and swiped away the wetness with his thumbs, a deep frown furrowing his brows. "Your parents . . . did they come and see you?"

"Not once," she said, her voice raspy from the painful sob she'd managed to hold back. "They never acknowledged the fact that I nearly died or came to visit me during my stay in rehab after it happened or joined me during my therapy sessions. Regret, sadness, shame, survivor's guilt . . . I went through it all alone."

"Ahh, sweetheart . . ." He slid his arms around her and pulled her into his embrace. "You're not alone anymore."

She wrapped her arms around his waist, her cheek resting on his warm chest as he stroked her back. "No, I'm not. I have Clay, Mason, Levi—"

He pulled back and stared deep into her eyes. So deep she wanted to drown in the emotion she saw there. "And me, Tara," he said with a fierce conviction she wanted so badly to believe. "You have *me*."

Yes, for now she did. And for now, it was enough. "Thank you."

His hands came back up to her face again, cradling her as if she were a piece of fine china. "You are one of the strongest, most resilient women I know . . . and

I'm fucking crazy about you," he added with a grin.

She laughed, grateful for the bit of humor that served to chase away the depressing memories. "I'm a little crazy about you, too," she admitted, unable to deny the butterflies in her stomach that accompanied that truthful statement.

"Spend the day with me," he insisted with a smile. "We can have lunch at Navy Pier, go to a movie, anything you want."

She wanted to say yes so badly but was instead filled with regret. "I can't. I have to be at work at four, and I close down the bar tonight."

His lips flattened into a sullen line. "Can I just say I hate your fucking schedule?" he grumbled unhappily.

For the first time ever, so did she. "Are you seriously pouting right now?"

"No," he insisted, though the small smirk that suddenly replaced his glum expression contradicted his denial. "I just want to make you, and us, work. I want to see you and date you and just . . . be with you."

Oh, this man made her heart all aflutter. "I want the same thing," she whispered.

"Then we'll figure out a way to make it work," he said as his hands dropped to her hips, then circled around to grab her ass, hauling her to the edge of the counter so the front zipper of his jeans was pressed tight against her sex.

"Okay," she agreed breathlessly.

"Good." He effortlessly picked her up, and she automatically wrapped her legs around his waist to hold on while he headed back toward her bedroom, then set her on the bed. "But for right now, since our time today is limited, I vote for spending it right here, between these gorgeous thighs of yours."

She bit her bottom lip as her body started to melt. "I vote for the same thing," she said as he pulled her shorts and panties off and did the same with her tank top.

"See?" he murmured, a pleased smile on his face as he settled between her spread legs, his mouth inches away from where she wanted him the most. "Look at how fucking compatible we are."

Her only answer was a compatible moan as he proceeded to show her in detail exactly how well they fit together.

Chapter Eleven

Have fun shopping with Samantha today. Buy some-thing sexy to wear to the party on Saturday that I'll have fun taking off later when we're alone.

TARA SMILED, HER heart feeling lighter than air as she read Jackson's sweet text. She was meeting Samantha in about an hour at a boutique in Chicago close to where she worked as a pastry chef. Since Jackson was taking Tara to an anniversary gala for his firm, where she was meeting his bosses and colleagues for the first time, she wanted Samantha to help her find something sophisticated and classy, with a subtle bit of sexy thrown in just for Jackson. She desperately wanted to make a good first impression, and that tiny insecure part of her wanted to fit in his upper-class world and be the respectable girlfriend he deserved on his arm. She wanted to make him proud.

She bit her bottom lip and replied. *Don't you know*

it's all about the anticipation of unwrapping the outer package and enjoying the surprise beneath... all in good time?

Jackson quickly texted back, *Can I unwrap you before the party? I promise to make it worth your while.*

She laughed. The man was incorrigible and insatiable. *Absolutely not. I'm not going to meet your bosses knowing you defiled me before we even left my house.*

Fine, but be warned that I plan to make up for it once we get back to my place.

She was already looking forward to it. *Fair enough.*

I've got a meeting to go to. I'll stop by Kincaid's tonight to see you at work.

Okay. TTYL. Tara hesitated, then before she changed her mind, she added a pink sparkly heart emoji to the end of her text—the first indication she'd ever given Jackson that her feelings for him were so much stronger than she'd been able to put into words.

Much to her surprise, he replied with a smiley face with heart eyes.

Silly as it was, her heart did a happy little dance. She set her phone down on her nightstand and finished getting dressed for her shopping expedition with Samantha.

Five weeks ago, and prior to meeting Jackson, Tara never would have thought she could fall in love with a man so quickly. But in those five weeks, Jackson Stone had definitely altered her emotions in the best way possible. In ways that made her heart feel full whenever she was with him and empty when they were apart.

He made her believe that fairy tales existed and made her hopeful for her own happily-ever-after, when she'd lived the past six years certain she didn't deserve that kind of bliss.

She actually saw a future with Jackson. Every moment that she spent with him made her more aware of how in sync they were and made her feel as though she'd found the one person who understood and accepted her, despite the mistakes she'd made in the past. He made her laugh, he made her feel beautiful, and he made her feel . . . whole. It certainly didn't hurt that the man was sexy as fuck and knew a dozen filthy ways to make her body hum with pleasure.

She loved that Jackson was forging a relationship with Clay, Mason, and Levi. He'd been upfront about the assault charge and what had happened, and the guys actually *apologized* for jumping to wrong conclusions. The Kincaid brothers were making a concentrated effort on their end to get to know Jackson, as well. Including learning about the past and the kind of childhood he'd had, which had been as troubled as their own.

They met for drinks at the bar at least once a week, and Jackson had invited them to a Cubs game at Wrigley Field, where his company sponsored one of the luxury suites over home plate. Yeah, the guys had been impressed, and Mason had even deemed his brother "a cool guy." And last Saturday, Clay had taken all of them to the Chicagoland Speedway for an afternoon of racing stock cars.

The brothers' growing relationship made Tara extremely happy, and she knew that Jackson was finally beginning to feel like maybe, possibly, he had a chance to fit into the Kincaid family.

Her cell phone on the nightstand vibrated, and, hoping it was another text from Jackson—yeah, she really did have it bad for him—she picked it up in anticipation and was surprised to see a message from Clay instead.

Could you come by Kincaid's before meeting Samantha? There's something I want to talk to you about.

She frowned as she finished reading the text. Clay sometimes came into the bar during the morning or early afternoon hours to check on things, but he'd never summoned her in the middle of the day, at least not without letting her know what, exactly, he wanted or needed. She wondered if she'd done something wrong, and tried not to read too much into his words.

She replied, *Sure. I'll be there in fifteen minutes.*

Tara grabbed her purse and headed out the door, and as soon as she arrived at Kincaid's, she walked inside and headed straight for Clay's office. He was sitting behind the desk doing something on the computer, and she knocked on the door to get his attention.

He glanced up, his unreadable features giving nothing away as he leaned back in his chair. "Come on in and sit down. This shouldn't take long."

Was that good or bad? She honestly couldn't tell.

She settled into one of the seats in front of his

desk. Now that she knew Jackson better, it was easy to see the differences, along with the similarities, in the twin brothers. They might have been separated at birth, but these two men possessed so many of the same qualities—loyalty and integrity being at the top of the list. Beyond their good looks, the inflections in their voices and the way they laughed were nearly identical, and they both frowned the same way when something was on their mind—very much like Clay's current expression.

"How are things with you and Jackson?" he asked.

His even tone of voice gave her no indication of where this line of questioning was heading, so she figured she'd just be honest and see where it led. "Really good. It's definitely hard working around our conflicting hours, but we're finding ways to spend time together." The evenings when she worked the late shift at the bar, Jackson accompanied her home to her place, and the nights she had off, she spent at his condo in the city. Not ideal, but they'd agreed that their flourishing relationship was worth the sacrifices they had to make to be with each other.

Clay nodded in understanding and rubbed his hand along his jaw. "I noticed you scheduled yourself off for this Saturday night."

Her body stiffened defensively before she could catch herself. "I'm going to an anniversary gala with Jackson. Is that a problem?"

A hint of amusement kicked up the corners of Clay's mouth, adding to her annoyance. "No. Not at all, so calm down."

She glared at him, because he obviously knew how anxious she was about this impromptu meeting. "Then stop being a jerk and dragging this out, and tell me, why am I here?"

"I was getting there," he said, and laughed. "I've made a decision about the bar that could work to your benefit. That is, if you're interested in my offer."

She shifted restlessly in her seat. "I'm listening." *So get on with it already!*

He sat forward in his chair and folded his hands on his desk, his gaze suddenly all business. "I've decided to open Kincaid's at eleven in the morning instead of four in the afternoon, to cater to a lunch crowd. Which means I'm going to need a day manager as well as a night manager, and I wanted to give you first choice of which shift you'd prefer. I figured your current schedule made it difficult for you to spend time with Jackson, so I'm hoping this might help you out."

Her jaw opened, then closed as a slow, ecstatic smile spread across her face. "Are you serious?"

He arched a brow, sarcasm glimmering in his eyes. "About opening the bar for lunch? Or offering you the day shift?"

It wasn't often that Clay was a smartass, but he was definitely enjoying himself a little too much. So she one-upped him. "Actually, are you serious about supporting a relationship between myself and Jackson?"

Clay had the decency to look contrite, considering how he and his brothers had treated Jackson when they'd first met him. But in the five weeks that Jackson had been a part of their lives, they'd come a long way in accepting their brother as part of their family.

"Look, I know Mason and Levi and I had some growing pains to go through when it came to Jackson," Clay said sincerely. "But we've spent enough time with him to see that he really is an upstanding guy, so we approve of the two of you dating."

She rolled her eyes derisively. "I'm so relieved that I have the Kincaid seal of approval."

"You're welcome." He grinned like a scoundrel. "So, what will it be? Day or night shift?"

The choice was an easy one to make. "I would love the day shift manager position."

"Consider it yours." Clay looked equally pleased. "It's going to take a few weeks to get everything in place before we make the change to include serving lunch. I'll start the process of interviewing applicants for the night shift, but I'd like you to start work at eleven beginning next week so you can help with everything to make it a smooth transition. We'll need to discuss more bartenders and waitresses, and I'm doing some menu options, as well."

She couldn't deny the way. "She glanced at thing new and differ food up. "I hate to cut degree to good use going so I'm not late the time on b this sho meeting up with Samantha."

"Go ahead and go. We'll talk more about this later."

Feeling like her life was finally falling into place, she turned around and headed for the door.

"Have fun dress shopping for the party with Jackson on Saturday."

She spun around at the realization that Clay had been jerking her chain earlier about taking a weekend night off. Her gaze narrowed on her boss while he gave her a not-so-innocent look. "You knew all along why I scheduled myself off on Saturday."

"Yeah, I knew. Samantha told me," he admitted, and smiled warmly at her. "You look happier than I've ever seen you, Tara, and I'm pretty sure Jackson is the reason."

"He is," she said softly, honestly.

Clay nodded. "That alone makes me like the guy, regardless of the fact that he's my brother and twin. You deserve someone who treats you like gold and ᵐakes you feel special, because you are."

ᵃ lump formed in her throat, because Clay wasn't his wᵥwax poetically, unless, of course, it came to Samantʰ̓ou've become a softie since marrying He sʰ

"There are t didn't deny her truthful claim. family, and yᵗ ᵖˡe I care about and consider if Jackson so ᵥᵖle them. But just so you know, announced that ᵗ hem. ᵧₒᵤ, Mason has already fucking kneecaps."

Clay had the decency to look contrite, considering how he and his brothers had treated Jackson when they'd first met him. But in the five weeks that Jackson had been a part of their lives, they'd come a long way in accepting their brother as part of their family.

"Look, I know Mason and Levi and I had some growing pains to go through when it came to Jackson," Clay said sincerely. "But we've spent enough time with him to see that he really is an upstanding guy, so we approve of the two of you dating."

She rolled her eyes derisively. "I'm so relieved that I have the Kincaid seal of approval."

"You're welcome." He grinned like a scoundrel. "So, what will it be? Day or night shift?"

The choice was an easy one to make. "I would love the day shift manager position."

"Consider it yours." Clay looked equally pleased. "It's going to take a few weeks to get everything in place before we make the change to include serving lunch. I'll start the process of interviewing applicants for the night shift, but I'd like you to start work at eleven beginning next week so you can help me with everything to make it a smooth transition. We'll need more bartenders and waitresses, and we can discuss menu options, as well."

She couldn't deny the excitement of doing something new and different and putting her business degree to good use. "Thank you, Clay." She glanced at the time on her cell phone and stood up. "I hate to cut this short, but I need to get going so I'm not late meeting up with Samantha."

"Go ahead and go. We'll talk more about this later."

Feeling like her life was finally falling into place, she turned around and headed for the door.

"Have fun dress shopping for the party with Jackson on Saturday."

She spun around at the realization that Clay had been jerking her chain earlier about taking a weekend night off. Her gaze narrowed on her boss while he gave her a not-so-innocent look. "You knew all along why I scheduled myself off on Saturday."

"Yeah, I knew. Samantha told me," he admitted, and smiled warmly at her. "You look happier than I've ever seen you, Tara, and I'm pretty sure Jackson is the reason."

"He is," she said softly, honestly.

Clay nodded. "That alone makes me like the guy, regardless of the fact that he's my brother and twin. You deserve someone who treats you like gold and makes you feel special, because you are."

A lump formed in her throat, because Clay wasn't a man to wax poetically, unless, of course, it came to his wife. "You've become a softie since marrying Samantha."

He shrugged but didn't deny her truthful claim. "There are certain people I care about and consider family, and you're one of them. But just so you know, if Jackson so much as hurts you, Mason has already announced that he will break his fucking kneecaps."

She laughed, because that was exactly something that Mason would say, and do, if needed.

SINCE TARA WAS running late because of her meeting with Clay, she sent a text to Samantha to meet her in front of the boutique instead of Adeline's, where Samantha worked. The other woman was already at the shop by the time Tara arrived. Her blonde hair was plaited into a neat French braid, and she was wearing a T-shirt with the Adeline's logo that molded to her increasingly growing belly. Samantha and Clay had recently announced that they were having a girl, and everyone couldn't be more excited to meet the newest member of the Kincaid family.

When Tara finally reached her friend, they hugged, then Samantha gave her a handled bag from the bakery. "I brought some freshly made cream puffs for you and that gorgeous man of yours," she said in a teasing tone. "Of course, I can get away with saying that since he looks exactly like Clay."

Tara laughed. This wasn't the first time that Samantha had brought her and Jackson treats she'd made. "You're spoiling Jackson. You know that, right?"

Samantha shrugged, an impish smile on her pink glossy lips. "I just want to make sure he feels welcome and like part of the family."

"He really does," Tara assured Samantha, appreciating her efforts. "And he's certainly not going to refuse a care package of pastries from you."

Since her car was parked nearby, Tara put the desserts into her vehicle, then came back and linked her arm through Samantha's as they walked toward the boutique.

"How are you feeling?" Tara asked. The other woman was glowing, but then again, Samantha was stunningly beautiful and always well put together, which was why Tara wanted her advice on an appropriate dress to wear.

"Much better now that the first trimester is out of the way," she admitted as she placed her hand on the taut swell of her stomach. "My morning sickness is gone, thank God, but now my hormones are wreaking havoc with my sex drive. I want it *all* the time. Every morning, every night, and oh, my God, the orgasms are so freakin' intense." She blushed.

"Lucky Clay," Tara teased as she opened the door for Samantha.

"Yeah, he's more than accommodating," she said cheerfully as she slipped past Tara, then added with a naughty twinkle in her eyes, "He says it's a tough job, but someone has to do it."

"Yeah, what a hardship," Tara said humorously.

They strolled into the shop, the clothing more unique and upscale compared to where Tara normally bought her clothes. Definitely more catered to Samantha's previous kind of lifestyle, before she'd walked away from her family's wealth for the man she loved. Clay had more than enough money to buy anything

Samantha's heart desired, but her wants and needs were simple and revolved around her husband, and now the baby they were going to have.

Tara came to a stop beside Samantha as the other woman eyed a mannequin wearing a sexy red dress with a plunging neckline. Her fingers touched the silky-looking material as she glanced at Tara.

"So, what are we looking for today?" she asked curiously. "Sophisticated or slutty?"

Tara laughed. "Definitely sophisticated. It's a huge gala to celebrate the firm's twenty-fifth anniversary, and it's being held at the Bridgeport Art Center."

Samantha raised an impressed brow. "Wow. Very swanky."

"I know," Tara breathed anxiously. "When I looked the place up on the Internet, I almost had a bona fide panic attack." It hadn't helped matters that Jackson told her there would probably be over four hundred people in attendance—from employees to clients to business associates in the industry.

"Really?" Samantha asked in surprise as she strolled to another dress hanging on a nearby rack—a black gown with gold trim that was too somber for Tara's tastes. "Why are you so nervous?"

Clearly, hanging out at grand, extravagant places like the Bridgeport Art Center was no big deal for someone like Samantha, who'd grown up in the lap of luxury and had attended events in the poshest and trendiest venues in the city. Tara, however, had not. In fact, she was certain she was going to be etiquette challenged compared to all the other cultured women present at the highfalutin party.

Tara tried to explain her apprehension. "Well, other than the art center being one of the most lavish places in the city, I'm sure I'm going to stick out like a sore thumb and look completely out of place."

"No, you're not." Samantha flashed her a confident smile. "That's why I'm here to help you."

"I'm meeting his bosses and colleagues for the first time, and I'd really like to make a good impression," she added, hating that her insecurities were getting the best of her, that her troubled past was messing with her head and instilling doubts.

She and Jackson had existed for the past five weeks in their own little bubble, surrounded by *her* friends and the people in *her* life. Everything had been easy and comfortable and familiar for *her*. This was the first time she was stepping outside of her safety zone with Jackson and into the sophisticated world in which he lived, including meeting influential co-workers, important friends, and clients who respected him as a man and architect. So yes, she was a bit frazzled by it all.

Samantha stopped perusing the store and turned to face Tara to give her her full attention. "Trust me," she said, her gaze soft and earnest as she squeezed one of Tara's hands. "By the time we're done here and we discuss your hair and makeup, you are going to look like a million bucks. No one will see you as anything other than the beautiful, stunning, woman on Jackson's arm. I promise."

Tara nodded, wanting to believe her friend. On the outside, she had no doubt that she'd look the part, but on the inside, she was still that young girl who'd been addicted to drugs and had overdosed, and a woman who feared she wasn't good enough for a successful man like Jackson.

"I just don't want to embarrass Jackson," she whispered, getting to the truth of the matter.

"Oh, honey, that's not possible," Samantha said in the sweetest, most genuine tone imaginable. "You are an amazing woman, and *he's* going to be the luckiest man at the gala with you by his side."

Tara appreciated Samantha's pep talk, and it made her realize that in order for Jackson to feel like that fortunate man at the gala who was proud to be with her, it all hinged on Tara's attitude and disposition. She needed to beat back her nerves and embrace the strong, confident, fearless woman she'd evolved into because of Jackson's influence.

He believed in her and wanted her there, and she was going to do everything in her power to make sure he didn't regret having her on his arm.

Chapter Twelve

JACKSON COULDN'T STOP staring at the most stunning woman at the party, and the fact that she was his date made him one hell of a lucky son of a bitch.

An hour into the reception part of the gala, and Tara was charming the pants off one of his clients, George Weber, a gentleman in his late seventies who owned a media firm and enjoyed mixed drinks. Jackson also knew that man enjoyed beautiful women— he'd been married four times and joked about finding a fifth wife. It didn't escape Jackson's notice that Weber had been completely captivated by Tara from the moment Jackson had introduced them.

Hell, there wasn't a man in the place who hadn't given her a second look, even if it was a subtle glance in her direction while their girlfriends or wives weren't paying attention. Jackson couldn't blame them. She was wearing a gorgeous, dark purple, calf-length dress that was sexy yet classy. Sexy because it molded to her curves, highlighting her full breasts and perfect ass. Classy because there was nothing blatant about what it revealed. The sheer stockings encasing her slender legs intrigued him, made him wonder where they ended and what else she was wearing beneath the dress. And the strappy stiletto heels on her feet . . . Jesus, they inspired all sorts of dirty fantasies, and he couldn't wait to fuck her in them later.

And her silky, shiny black hair . . . he preferred it down because he liked having those soft strands tangling around his hands, but there was something so provocative about seeing it in an intricate, upswept style that left her shoulders bare and exposed her slender neck. The pearls around her throat that she'd borrowed from Samantha, along with a matching cuff bracelet, completed the elegant, sophisticated look.

When he'd arrived to pick her up at her place, she'd been about to remove the diamond stud above her lip because she'd been worried that it wasn't appropriate in such an upscale setting, that some people might make not-so-nice assumptions about her based on an unconventional type of piercing.

His response to that concern of hers? *"I don't give a damn what other people think. I don't want you to hide anything about yourself, and I fucking love that piercing, so it stays."*

She hadn't looked one hundred percent convinced, but she'd left the diamond in place, even though he knew just how difficult that had been for her to do.

When he'd first mentioned taking her to the gala, she'd admitted that being in such a luxurious environment made her nervous. That she was worried about fitting in, of people taking one look at her and judging her. That she'd mess up and say or do something that would embarrass him. So far, all she'd done was impress the hell out of Jackson with her willingness to try, while trusting that he'd be right there to support her.

After George had gallantly kissed the back of Tara's hand, he'd asked what she did for work. Because Jackson had his hand touching her lower back, he'd felt the slight stiffening of her body that told him she was uncomfortable admitting she was a bartender when it was obvious that most of the ladies at the gala were either high-powered career women or wealthy trophy wives. But the moment she'd answered George—very confidently, Jackson was proud to say—the other man had been fascinated, and a conversation about all his favorite liquors and cocktails had ensued.

Currently, they were bantering back and forth as George tried to stump Tara with an alcoholic beverage she'd never heard of before. Most were old-timers' drinks, and so far Tara was holding her own. While Jackson had never heard of a Whiskey Smash, a Rusty Nail, or a Sidecar, Tara rattled off the ingredients like a pro, and George was impressed with her knowledge.

Jackson introduced Tara to the owners of Schmidt and Kramer, along with the other partners and their wives, who were all gracious and welcoming. With over four hundred people in attendance, the venue was full, and mingling was difficult, but with Tara's hand tucked securely in his arm, Jackson tried to make the rounds to say hello to as many of his clients and colleagues as he could.

They sat through a five-course dinner, chatted with the other guests at their table, and listened to a speech the owners of the company made expressing their appreciation to their employees and clients, acknowledging their commitment to the industry, and sharing their goals to expand into a more global marketplace. Afterward, Jackson pulled Tara out to the dance floor just so he had time alone with her and could hold her close during a slow song. He wrapped an arm around her waist and tucked one of her hands against his chest, right over the heart that was quickly becoming hers.

He knew it was a huge statement, but five weeks with Tara had given him a renewed outlook on his life. He'd gone from being a man who'd felt like an outcast to feeling as though he'd finally found the one person who filled the emptiness inside him that he'd carried his entire life. She understood his past struggles and his pain, because she'd been there herself and knew what it was like being an outsider in her own family. She complemented him in every way that mattered, and because of Tara, he finally felt as though he was exactly where he belonged, with the person he was truly meant to be with.

Life was good and he couldn't have been more content or satisfied personally or professionally. But it was in perfect moments like this that a small, contrary part of Jackson's subconscious reminded him that nothing good in his life lasted forever. And it was that deeply instilled fear that kept him from telling Tara how he truly felt about her. That he loved her, more than he'd ever believed he could love another person. That she alone made him feel whole and complete.

He was so fucking afraid that everything would disappear if he spoke the words out loud, that this happiness he'd finally found with her, and with his brothers, would vanish and he'd be left picking up the pieces all over again. His entire life had been that way, a sequence of unexpected disappointments and realizing that nothing had ever been as it had seemed. Just when he was confident and hopeful about his future, as he was right now, that other proverbial shoe dropped and kicked him in the ass.

But fuck... he desperately wanted this time around with Tara to be different. But the thought of potentially losing her kept him from saying the words that had the ability to change everything between them. Not knowing if that declaration would alter their relationship for the better or worse was what held him back.

"Hey, if you squeeze me any tighter, I'm not going to be able to breathe," Tara said, her voice soft and laced with humor.

Jesus, he hadn't realized he was crushing her body

to his, that deep-seated fear manifesting its way into his reality. "Sorry," he muttered on a harsh exhale, and loosened his hold around her waist so that his hand rested on the curve of her hip.

She tipped her head to the side, her gaze suddenly concerned as she searched his face. "Is everything okay? You seem tense all of a sudden."

He forced himself to relax and smiled at her. "Everything is fine," he promised, and deliberately shoved all those dismal thoughts from his head to focus on the here and now and the woman in his arms. "How are *you* doing?"

"I'm doing great."

She returned his smile, but Jackson knew her changing expressions well enough by now to know that beneath her upbeat reply, she was overwhelmed by the evening's festivities. After nearly four hours of mingling, being introduced to dozens of people, and making polite chitchat, he suspected she was pretty close to her limit. Hell, *he* was exhausted and decided after the song ended, it was time for them to go. He was done sharing her tonight.

She idly skimmed her hand down the lapel of his black suit jacket, then touched her fingers to the purple tie she'd given him when he'd arrived to pick her up, so that they'd match. "I don't think I've had the chance to tell you how dashing you look in your suit tonight," she said flirtatiously.

"And you look absolutely stunning," he replied honestly. "Easily the most beautiful woman in the room."

Her cheeks flushed pink as she arched a brow. "You do realize that flattery isn't required to get laid tonight, right?"

He chuckled. "It's the truth, sweetheart. Your sexy dress, your elegant hairstyle that I can't wait to dishevel with my fingers . . ." Leaning closer, he pressed his lips to her ear and whispered seductively, "And those indecently hot fuck-me shoes that are driving my cock insane with thoughts of you wearing them while I—"

Tara jerked back and pressed her hand over his mouth, her eyes wide in shock, though there was no denying the flicker of desire glimmering in the depths. "You can't say those kinds of dirty things at a work function," she scolded in a low voice. "What if one of your bosses or a client hears you?"

He shrugged and dragged her hand away from his lips. "Hey, I'm just expressing my appreciation for how exquisite you look tonight."

She laughed, then her features turned more wistful. "What you see right now isn't really me," she said of the fancy dress, the elaborate hair, the extraneous embellishments. "To be honest, I kind of feel like Cinderella at the ball."

Like a fraud and someone who didn't belong. He could easily read between the lines, and he hated that she'd think of herself that way. He understood that his work situation was different from hers, that as an architect, he was more entrenched in an affluent social circle, while she was a bartender who served a middle-class crowd, but this gala didn't represent the man he was, nor did it reflect the things he wanted in his life.

He loved his career, and having nice things was definitely a bonus, but he knew, without a doubt, that none of it mattered if he ended up spending the rest of his life alone. Or without her by his side.

He released her, and, uncaring of who might see, he framed her face in his hands and made sure she was looking directly into his eyes so she could see everything he felt for her reflecting in his gaze. "Sweetheart, this isn't some kind of fairy tale that goes away when the clock strikes midnight," he told her gently, aware of the irony. He'd been dealing with the same fears himself. "It's you and me together, and it's as real as it gets. Don't ever doubt that."

There was no missing the undeniable relief he saw in her expression, as if his words had alleviated her doubts—and that consoled him, as well.

He released his hold on her face and gave her a wicked grin. "So, are you ready to blow this joint and move on to more pleasurable activities?"

Her beautiful blue eyes lit up with excitement as she batted her lashes playfully at him. "Are you propositioning me, Mr. Stone?"

"Fuck yes," he growled in a low, suddenly impatient tone of voice so the people dancing nearby couldn't hear. "Is it working?"

"Oh, yeah," she agreed as she gave his tie a playful tug that made his dick twitch in anticipation. "Take me back to your place so I can show you exactly what I'm wearing, or *not* wearing, beneath this dress."

✧   ✧   ✧

TARA WALKED INTO Jackson's modern, stylish condo on Lake Shore Drive, a far cry from her tiny home that looked old and outdated in comparison. No matter how many times she'd been to his place, she was always in awe of the sleek furnishings, the hardwood flooring, and the gorgeous open floor plan that led straight into a spacious living room. While Jackson switched on a lamp to give the room some light, then shrugged off his suit jacket and slipped off his tie, she strolled behind the leather couch, gravitating to the floor-to-ceiling windows that overlooked the city from thirty-five stories up.

She stood there, taking in the peaceful sight. The view at night was always so spectacular and a bit magical to her. It was as if she and Jackson were in their own little world, and the only thing that existed outside of his place were starry, shimmering lights and the promise of forever.

He came up behind her, settled his hands on her waist, and placed a warm kiss on the nape of her neck still exposed by her upswept hair. The touch of his lips elicited a shiver of delight and tightened her breasts, her body easily submitting to whatever this man wanted to do to her. They'd talked about the gala on the drive back to his place, about the clients she'd met and some interesting conversations they'd had, but now that they were completely alone, Tara wanted the rest of the night to be just about the two of them.

He nuzzled the side of her throat and traced his hands up her sides, then settled them flat against her rib cage. "So, about what you're wearing or not wearing beneath this dress, I'm definitely curious to find out."

She bit her bottom lip as his thumbs brushed beneath the undersides of her aching breasts, teasing her, arousing her. "Then unzip me so you can see for yourself," she murmured, shifting anxiously on the stiletto heels strapped to her feet.

"Right *here*?" he asked scandalously.

She smiled, remembering one night a few weeks ago when he'd stripped her bare in front of these windows, and she'd been so shocked and uncertain, and yeah, a bit of modesty had kicked in. But he'd promised that no one could see into the living room since they were too high up and there were no other buildings directly in front of his.

She'd been skeptical, and it had taken some coaxing and major seduction on his part to get her to relax and not feel like an exhibitionist. But once he knew that he had her full consent, he'd placed her hands on the window and ordered her to keep them there, then smacked her ass with his palm—and not playfully, either. He'd spanked each cheek until her flesh was hot and tingling and her pussy was pulsing for release. And it wasn't until she begged that he finally pressed her upper body against the glass as he fucked her from behind and straight into a screaming orgasm.

It had been one of the hottest, most thrilling sexual experiences of her life. *So far.* With Jackson, there was no telling what kind of depraved kink he'd introduce her to, but he'd yet to let her down.

He was still waiting for her answer, and she didn't disappoint him. "Yes, right here."

"Look at you," he said, his tone impressed as he gradually lowered the zipper down her back as she gazed out at the city. "I think my dirty girl likes the thought of other people watching."

Only when she *knew* there was no one watching, she thought in amusement. But her mind couldn't deny it was a potent fantasy that got her off.

His warm hands slid over her now bare shoulders, skimming the sleeves of her dress down her arms to her waist. He pushed the rest of the material over her hips and let it drop to the floor at her feet. He was still standing behind her and slightly to the side so he could look at the window and see the front of her body reflecting in the glass.

"No bra," he said on a groan while the fingers of one hand brushed along her spine, causing her breasts to swell and tighten even more. "How the fuck did I not know this *all night long?*"

Surprise, she thought with a wicked smile of her own. It wasn't often she could get one up on this man, and it was fun to see his shock. "The dress has a built-in bra, so there's no need to wear one."

He grabbed one of her hands and helped her step out of the pool of fabric on the ground so she didn't trip over it in her heels, then led her back around the couch until she was standing a few feet away from the sofa. As she watched, he removed the cufflinks on his white dress shirt, set them on a nearby side table, then finished unfastening the rest of the buttons down the front. He shrugged out of the shirt and draped it over a chair, toed off his shoes and took off his socks, then strolled over to the leather couch.

She'd expected him to sit on the sofa like he normally did, but instead he lowered himself to the hardwood floor so he was sitting with his back braced against the front of the couch.

"What are you doing?" she asked curiously.

He unfastened his pants, lowered the zipper, and pushed his briefs down just enough to free his already thick, hard erection. "I'm making myself comfortable," he said with a smirk.

"I would think that sitting on the sofa would be much more comfortable than the hard floor," she said, still confused.

"I'm leaving room on the couch for *you* to be comfortable." The sinful gleam in his eyes told her that whatever he had in mind tonight, it probably wasn't going to be anything less than mind-blowingly erotic.

He hadn't told her she could move, and knowing the kind of games he liked to play—the kind where he dominated and she submitted—she patiently waited for his next order.

His heated gaze took a leisurely journey down her body, taking in her naked breasts, the lacy black panties she was wearing, the thigh-high stockings encasing her legs, and the black strappy heels on her feet. Her body felt flushed from his scorching perusal. The cock he'd released from his pants twitched, but he didn't touch his erection as he just as slowly lifted his eyes back up to her face.

"Take all the pins out of your hair," he ordered in a raspy voice.

Lifting her hands, she started plucking the pins that held the intricate design of her hair in place. It seemed like such an intimate thing to do, and it made her feel luxuriously sensual. With him watching as every wavy strand of hair she released fell around her shoulders and down her back, she thought about the present she had for him.

"So, I have a surprise for you," she said as another wavy length of hair cascaded down her chest, and the ends curled around her nipple like a kiss.

He stared enviously at that piece of hair and licked his lips, as if he wanted to be the one to touch his tongue to the budding tip. For as effortlessly as this man could seduce her, it was moments like these that made her realize just how much power she had over him, how easily she could influence and bewitch him by just doing whatever he asked.

"I can't imagine anything better than what I'm looking at right now." His hand moved to his shaft, and his fingers wrapped tight around the girth and stroked the length. "You are a fucking goddess."

She tried to keep her mind focused, which wasn't

easy to do when the sight of him slowly, leisurely pumping his cock through his hand turned *her* on just as much as it did him. "A month ago, right after the first time we were together, I had my doctor put me on birth control." Done pulling all the pins from her hair, she set them on the table with his cufflinks, then sifted her fingers through the strands to dishevel them a bit. "How do you feel about fucking me without a condom?"

His body visibly shuddered and he groaned. He squeezed his erection, and a drop of fluid beaded on the tip of his shaft, which he brushed away with his thumb.

He glanced up at her with a stupid-happy grin on his face. "That is the best fucking surprise ever."

She laughed, then sighed. "Men are *so* easy."

"Guilty," he admitted unabashedly, then his gaze turned serious. "Just so you know, I had my yearly right before we met, and I'm clean. I'd never risk you that way."

"I know." And she meant it. She trusted Jackson irrevocably with her body . . . it was her heart that she was having a more difficult time handing over to him. But that was her own doubts and insecurities to deal with. Her feelings for Jackson were stronger than anything she'd ever experienced before. She just needed to find the courage to take that one last leap of faith with him. *Soon.*

He widened his legs and bent his knees slightly, then crooked his finger at her. "Come here, Tara."

She strolled forward, putting a deliberate sway in her hips that he didn't miss, and stopped when she was standing right between his spread legs. He let go of his cock and skimmed his hands up both her stockinged legs. When he reached the lacy bands around her thighs, he brushed his fingertips over that exposed strip of flesh and up to the sides of her panties that rode low on her hips.

He hooked his thumbs into the elastic band. "You won't be needing these," he said with a lascivious grin as he gradually dragged the lacy scrap of fabric down her legs and bared the most intimate part of her. "The stockings and heels stay on."

He lifted one foot, then the other, removing her underwear and tossing it aside. Then he positioned one stiletto by his right hip and the other on his left, so she stood above him, her legs braced apart . . . the lips of her sex parted so that he could see, well, everything.

A few weeks ago, she would have been dying of embarrassment, but watching the desperate way he fisted his hard cock, along with the fog of lust etching his expression, had her pulse beating harder, faster, and need and arousal simmering through her veins.

"Fucking perfect," he said on a low, hungry growl that made her shiver in response. He put his head back on the couch cushion, resting it there, his eyes still open and trained on hers. "Come up onto the couch, sweetheart, and put your knees on either side of my head. I want my mouth and tongue on your pussy."

The breath seemed to collapse from her lungs. Just when she thought she had this man figured out, or he'd tapped out with every sexual trick in the book, he managed to add another level of eroticism to the mix.

His hands slid up the backs of her legs, urging her forward, his eyes hot and filled with the promise of ecstasy. The kind that would have her moaning and trembling in no time flat because he was *that* good. There was no resisting him and what he wanted, so she didn't even try—and who was she kidding, anyway? She was already halfway to an orgasm at the mere thought of what he was about to do to her—so she went ahead and knelt right above that decadent mouth of his, grabbed on to the back of the sofa for support, and prepared herself for his brand of possession.

Normally, he liked to tease and draw out her climax, but tonight she felt a definite urgency in the way he gripped her hips to hold her in place, an undeniable hunger as he fastened his mouth between her thighs and sank his tongue deep into her slick folds. She gasped as he licked along her cleft, then settled right over her clit. Her entire body jolted as he sucked the sensitive nub in his mouth and plied it with soft swirls of his tongue. *Again and again and again . . .*

The desire spiraling in her belly, and lower, coiled tighter and tighter. The intensity of his mouth overwhelmed her. He went at her harder, faster, deeper, ruthless in his attempt to claim her acquiescence, and she was helpless to deny what he was demanding from her: her complete and total surrender.

Giving herself over to Jackson was incredibly easy to do. Trusting him was like jumping over a cliff knowing there was a safety net to catch her, and she didn't think twice about letting go. Another deep, open-mouth, tongue-thrusting kiss against her pussy and she was panting, moaning, writhing, pleading . . . then crying out as her orgasm sent her free-falling over the edge while Jackson groaned in lust and satisfaction against her tender flesh.

He didn't give her time to recover before he was pulling her off the couch and guiding her down to straddle his lap. His fingers clutched her hips almost painfully, and she inhaled a sharp breath as he plunged inside of her in one deep, endless stroke, burying himself to the hilt. She expected him to unleash his own passion, was more than prepared to take the brunt of the volatile storm she felt brewing inside of him—even though she wasn't sure why. But instead he stilled, his chest heaving, his entire body taut with restraint. He was clearly holding himself back, as if he was afraid he'd hurt her if he let go, and it was the last thing she wanted.

His eyes were dark pools of need; his lips shone with moisture *from her*. It was so damn hot that she framed his face in her hands and bent her head to lick the taste of her from his mouth. "Do it, Jackson," she whispered against his lips, softly, imploringly. "Fuck me as hard as you need to and make me yours."

The sound that erupted from his chest was raw and primal as he wrapped his arms tight around her, then shifted and rolled her to her back so that she was lying on the bare hardwood floor and he was on top of her, already sinking back inside of her, impaling her as if he owned her while shoving her legs far apart to make room for him in between.

And still, it didn't seem to be enough. He slid his hands up her back and clamped his fingers around her shoulders, anchoring her in place as his hips slammed hard against hers, and there was nowhere she could go, nothing she could do but let him take her, however he wanted. However he needed. His chest crushed against her breasts, and he melded his mouth to hers, his body completely dominating hers with long, frantic, aggressive, grinding thrusts.

It would be easy to write this off as just rough, animal sex, but Tara knew better. The emotion pouring off of him was nearly tangible. He couldn't seem to get deep enough, couldn't seem to get close enough, as if he were trying to fuse their bodies, their souls. As if he was afraid of losing her . . . and it was a feeling she recognized and understood all too well.

She finally, *finally*, felt that control of his break. His thrusts grew more erratic—shorter, harder, deeper jerks of his hips that made her second release peak just as his did, her body convulsing and clenching around his cock. He tossed his head back, his jaw clenched, teeth bared as he came on a long, endless moan that vibrated through her.

Completely spent, he collapsed on top of her and buried his face against her neck, and she caressed her hands down the slope of his back as they both spent a few extra minutes recovering from the intensity of their orgasms.

All that Tara cared about in that moment was they were joined, connected, and inseparable. They had plenty of time to figure out the rest.

Chapter Thirteen

Since you have the day off, would you like to come by my office around one? I'd love to show you around and take you to lunch.

JACKSON SENT THE text off to Tara, then set his phone on his desk as he went back to reviewing the construction documents for an upcoming commercial design he'd been assigned as project manager. He had a three o'clock meeting with the CEO and CFO of the company and wanted to make sure he was prepared to answer any questions that might arise.

But from one to three this afternoon, he had a two-hour window of time. Normally, he had lunch appointments with clients, but today he was free for that short period. And since, for the past week, Tara had been working her ass off with Clay to get everything prepared to now cater for a lunch crowd at Kincaid's, their time together had been limited. She'd been exhausted in the evenings, and he'd worked late a couple of nights. Their schedules were still conflicting more than he liked, and it just seemed like something was a bit off with Tara. Then again, she'd always held a part of herself back—not physically but emotionally. And he couldn't deny that it worried him. A lot.

He chalked it up to her being overworked and tired, and while he'd like to think that a lunch date would get them back on track, he'd come to the decision that they were at a point in their relationship where he needed to trust his instincts. The intuition that had been telling him for weeks now that this woman was his soul mate—but he'd allowed insecurities and fears to get in the way. Tara was the one person who gave him everything he'd ever wanted. Everything he'd ever needed. A sense of belonging and the kind of unconditional acceptance he'd searched his entire life for.

He wanted those last bits of uncertainties between them gone, and he planned to replace them with genuine reassurances. After six weeks together, she deserved a solid commitment going forward, something to prove that he wasn't going anywhere. He definitely had his own hang-ups, along with a past that was filled with nothing but heartache and disappointments, but he knew that without taking a risk, there was no gain. And sweet, honest, fiercely loyal Tara Kent was worth taking that risk with his heart one last time. He'd be an idiot to let a woman like her slip through his fingers.

His phone vibrated with Tara's response. *Sure. That sounds good. I'll be there in just a bit.*

He leaned back in his chair and smiled to himself. Perfect. He'd give her a quick tour around the office to meet the few people they'd missed at the gala, then take her to the cafe down the street for a nice lunch. He was going to invite her to dinner this evening at his place, and by the time the night was over, she was going to know exactly how he felt about her. *That he loved her.*

With the decision made, he tried to focus on work until his secretary, Georgia, announced through the intercom that Tara was there to see him. He closed out the document on his computer, picked up this cell phone, and headed out to the reception area.

Tara had already met Georgia at the party, and the two were making small talk as he arrived. She'd worn a pretty cream-colored dress that ended below the knee and was trimmed in ruffles along the hem. She looked casual but tasteful, with her dark hair down in loose waves and her makeup lightly applied.

Without questioning the public display of affection, he walked right up to Tara and kissed her cheek as if she already belonged to him. Soon, she would.

"Hey, sweetheart," he said, and smiled at the blush that tinged her cheek.

"Hi," she replied, her blue eyes soft with her own subtle affection for him.

"You two are so cute together," Georgia said with a grin. "It's nice to see Jackson so smitten with a woman."

"I'm totally smitten," he admitted, uncaring of how that infatuation might make him look or sound because, well, he *was* crazy about her.

The phone on Georgia's desk rang, and she excused herself to take the call.

Jackson touched his hand to Tara's back and gently guided her toward his office. "Let me show you around and then we'll go grab a bite to eat."

"Sounds good."

Since it was lunchtime, the place was quieter than usual. He showed her his office, the conference room that they'd dubbed "the war room," and pointed out the photos on the hallway walls that showcased some of the projects he'd worked on. She seemed genuinely interested and impressed with the architectural aspect of his job and asked more questions than he'd anticipated. But the one thing he did realize was that he liked sharing this integral part of himself with her, and he loved that her enthusiasm was so authentic and real.

They reached the executive area of Schmidt and Kramer, where the president and vice-president of the company had a small suite of offices. Their admin secretary, Brynn Howell, took her lunch at eleven, so she was sitting behind her desk now, working away on her computer. The two main doors to the executive offices behind Brynn were open, and Jackson gave an amicable nod of acknowledgement to the men sitting inside each of those rooms, Walter Schmidt and Phillip Kramer. The two gentlemen did the same and smiled when they saw that Tara was with him, and she smiled and sent them a quick, friendly wave in silent greeting.

"Hi, Brynn," Jackson said as he grabbed Tara's hand as they approached the other woman's desk. "Since you missed the big anniversary party last weekend because you had the flu, I'd like you to meet my girlfriend."

When Brynn glanced up from her computer screen, he felt a slight resistance in Tara along with a sudden stiffening of her body and chalked it up to her normal unease in being introduced to yet another one of his colleagues. He would have thought after being surrounded by so many people in the industry at the gala, Tara would have been more comfortable meeting the people he worked with.

"Brynn, this is Tara Kent," he said, waving a hand between the two women. "Tara, this is Brynn Howell."

Jackson watched in confusion as Brynn stared at Tara in unmistakable shock. Neither one of the women spoke for what felt like the longest time, the tension between them nearly palpable, until Tara finally broke the strained silence between them.

"Brynn," Tara acknowledged tentatively, her wide blue eyes filled with uncertainty. "How are you?"

Brynn stood up but didn't answer, the animosity transforming her features surprising in its intensity before she glanced back at Jackson. "You're *dating* her?"

Beside Jackson, Tara flinched at the hostility behind the words. He frowned as he looked between the two women, trying to make sense of what was unfolding in front of him.

"Do the two of you know one another?" he asked, suddenly feeling as though he was chartering a very rocky, emotional terrain.

"If you count the fact that she's the drug addict who killed my brother, then yes, I know her," she said, bitterness dripping from her voice. "I can't believe someone like you is dating *her*. She's nothing but trash."

Jackson was so stunned by Brynn's heated outburst that he was rendered momentarily speechless. It was a side to her he'd never seen before.

"Brynn . . ." Tara's hand fluttered up to her throat. "I'm so sorry."

"You're *sorry*?" A caustic laugh escaped the other woman. "You're the one who should have died that day, not Michael. And now you're trying to be someone you're not and insinuating yourself into a decent man's life." She turned to Jackson. "Mark my words. She'll drag you into the gutter with her and ruin your life," she said before spinning around and walking out on Tara without another word.

Oh, shit. It was as if he'd been hit by a train as it finally dawned on Jackson who Brynn was to Tara, but before he could respond or check on her, Walter came out of his office and moved toward them. "Is something wrong out here?" he asked brusquely, one part concerned, another clearly upset by the disturbance.

Tara shook her head. "I'm sorry," she choked out

and darted down the hall before Jackson could stop her.

Jackson took a step, intending to go after her, but Walter called his name. Jackson barely heard the man's questions, and he quickly wrapped up the conversation, assuring him everything was fine. With his head spinning with *what the fuck just happened*, he rushed to find Tara and found her out by the elevators, frantically pushing the down button.

"Tara, stop," he said, his voice harsher than he'd intended, a direct result of the panic flowing through his veins.

The elevator doors slid open, and when she moved to bolt inside, he grabbed her arm and held her back, not wanting her to leave like this.

"Jackson, I have to go," she pleaded, her voice as distressed as the angst in her tear-filled eyes. "I *need* to go."

"And I need you to talk to me," he said firmly, trying like hell to ignore the pounding of his heart. "What just happened back there?" He had a general idea, but this extreme reaction of hers worried him the most. Along with the fact that she was running *away*. From him.

She shook her head, the agonized expression on her face nearly killing him. "I don't belong here."

"What do you mean, *here*?"

"With you," she said as those tears gathering in her eyes started rolling down her cheeks. "Brynn is right. You deserve someone better than me. I don't fit into this world of yours and I never will."

"Tara, that isn't true."

"Yes, it is. Don't you see? I'll never be free of my past. The terrible choices I made and the consequences I'll live with forever. You deserve better than someone whose actions will come back to embarrass you in front of your colleagues and your boss. Someone who *belongs* in your world." She choked out the words and hit the button to call the elevator once again.

The doors slid open a second time, and a blinding desperation clawed at him. "Tara—"

She stepped into the elevator just as Georgia came out of the office appearing genuinely contrite that she was interrupting him. "Jackson, I'm really sorry, but the call from Giles Patterson that you've been waiting for all morning is on line two."

Fuck. Jackson clenched his jaw in frustration as his gaze locked with Tara's as she stood inside the elevator, leaving him torn between what he *wanted* to do and what he *had* to do. It was an important phone call, potentially worth a fifty-million-dollar contract, and he couldn't blatantly ignore Patterson or put him off. It would be career suicide to blow off a man of his caliber. Hell, even if Jackson had gone to lunch with Tara, he would have excused himself to take the call.

"Jackson?" Georgia said from behind him, forcing him to make a decision right then.

His gut churned at the choice he knew he had to make. As the doors to the elevator started to slide closed and he saw the anguish in her expression, Jackson prayed he wasn't about to make a huge mistake he'd come to regret later.

"We're not done, Tara," he said gruffly, and then she was gone.

He meant what he'd said. Jackson wasn't giving Tara up without the fight of his life. However, it remained to be seen whether or not she would calm down and come around.

TARA DIDN'T KNOW where to go or who to turn to. She drove away from the office building where Jackson worked, her eyes blurry from her uncontrollable tears and her heart feeling as though it had just been cracked wide open and she'd never be the same again. Finding out that Brynn Howell worked at the same firm that Jackson did had been a definite shock to Tara's system. The loathing and contempt that the other woman still held toward Tara for Michael's death had been crushing.

But it had been Brynn's harsh words that had slapped Tara in the face and validated all her greatest fears—that she'd never be good enough for a respectable, honorable man like Jackson. Her shameful past wasn't something she could erase, and it would forever haunt her. She was also well aware that Jackson's relationship with an ex–drug addict could potentially taint his reputation for making such questionable choices in the women he dated. She wasn't the socially acceptable choice, she never would be, and there was no way she ever wanted to hurt Jackson or the career that meant so much to him.

She was an emotional mess and needed someone to talk to so she could clear her head and get a fresh perspective on the situation. She considered going to see Samantha, but she didn't want to risk running into Clay on her day off, so instead she drove to Mason's tattoo shop in hopes that Katrina was there.

Parking her car in an empty slot in front of Inked, she wiped away the moisture still on her cheeks and tried to gather her frayed composure. She glanced into the rearview mirror and cringed because she looked like crap. Her eyes were red and swollen, her skin ruddy since she'd smeared away most of her makeup. But it wasn't as though she was trying to impress anyone, so she got out of her vehicle and made her way inside the shop.

As soon as Katrina saw her, the other woman knew something was wrong. Her brows furrowed in concern as she grabbed Tara's hands and asked one simple question—*what's wrong?*—and Tara burst into a fresh batch of tears that left her sobbing and all her insecurities bubbling to the surface all over again.

"It's . . . it's Jackson," she finally managed to say, embarrassed that a few of the clients in Inked had seen her meltdown.

Katrina opened her mouth to reply, but a deep, terse, masculine voice beat her to it.

"What did the asshole do?" Mason demand to

know as he came out of his cubicle and walked toward the two of them. His shrewd gaze took in Tara's tear-stained face and her devastated expression, and his entire body tensed.

"He didn't do anything," she said, defending him before Mason could leap to all kinds of wrong assumptions. And that was the crux of it all. None of this was Jackson's fault. It was truly on her.

Mason jammed his hands on his hips, a fierce scowl shifting across his features. "Doesn't fucking look like *nothing* to me."

Katrina pursed her lips in annoyance. "Back off, He-Man," she told her husband. "She doesn't need you going all caveman on her behalf. Sometimes a girl just needs another woman to talk to, no violence necessary."

Mason didn't look completely convinced, his protective stance not relaxing one bit. "I already warned Jackson that I'd kick his ass if he ever hurt Tara, and the fact that you're crying and upset is enough to tell me that he did something stupid."

"I swear he didn't hurt me," Tara said adamantly so Mason would calm down. If anything, *she'd* hurt Jackson or, at the very least, had embarrassed him in front of his bosses. By now, she was sure the entire firm knew of her involvement in Brynn's brother's overdose and death, and she just hoped that the bad decisions she'd made in the past didn't do any damage to Jackson's career or reputation.

"It's what *I* did, not him," she admitted quietly.

Mason shook his head, looking utterly perplexed. "I don't get it."

"You don't need to get it," Katrina said, because clearly, she *did* understand.

He rolled his eyes at his wife. "Women are so fucking confusing," he grumbled, and stalked back to his workstation.

"Come on," Katrina said gently as she looped her arm in Tara's. "Let's go to the office, where it's quiet and private and we can talk without a certain someone butting in and adding his two cents to the conversation."

"I heard that," Mason shouted from his cubicle.

"I meant for you to," Katrina shot back without remorse as they walked toward the office.

The exchange made Tara smile, which she needed badly. She was also incredibly grateful for the alone time with her friend. Once they entered the office, Tara sat down in one of the small chairs, and Katrina made herself comfortable on the desk right in front of her.

"So, what happened?" Katrina asked, her tone kind and caring.

The whole incident poured out of Tara, the horrific confrontation with Brynn, the fact that Jackson's bosses had overheard the entire encounter and now knew all about her shameful and humiliating past, and how she'd ended things because a man like Jackson deserved so much better than what she had to offer.

"Wait a second," Katrina said, stopping Tara right

there. "First of all, what, exactly, are you *offering* Jackson at this point in the relationship? Besides sex, that is," she added with a knowing grin.

"I'm not sure what you mean," Tara said, trying to follow her friend's line of questioning.

Katrina curled her fingers around the edge of the desk and casually swung her legs back and forth. "Well, you said that Jackson deserved better than what you had to offer. Is the only thing you have to offer him sex? Or is there . . . more?"

She knew what Katrina was asking, and the ache in her heart made itself known. "Definitely more, at least for me." She swallowed hard and said the words out loud for the first time. "I love him." Unconditionally. Irrevocably.

Katrina's green eyes softened. "Have you told him?"

"No," she whispered, hating that her insecurities, and the fear of rejection, had kept her from opening her heart to him.

Katrina tipped her head to the side, studying Tara too insightfully. "So, what you have to offer Jackson is love, the one thing he's been searching for his entire life, yet you've decided to withhold it from him. Because he deserves better?" she asked incredulously. "Don't you think you should put all your emotional cards on the table and let Jackson be the judge of that?"

God, Katrina was right, yet . . . "What if . . . he doesn't feel the same way?"

"I don't think that's possible," Katrina said with a soft, knowing smile. "Not judging by the way he treats you and looks at you. But you won't know until you take a chance and get your feelings out in the open. He's a good man, Tara. We all know it and see it. Well, it took the guys a little longer to get their shit together in that department," she said with a laugh. "But even Mason has told me that Jackson belongs in this family not because he was born a Kincaid but because he possesses all those qualities that *make* him a Kincaid."

Tara already knew what those traits were, even without asking. Honesty. Integrity. Being loyal and passionate and protective. So many of the things she loved about him. Things she wanted and needed from a man in her life.

"But what if—"

Katrina shook her head, cutting Tara off. "No buts. Don't get so caught up in the past that you can't see the woman you are today. I almost made that mistake myself, and it nearly cost me my best friend and the man I love," she said of Mason, her husband and the love of her life. "You're no longer that defiant, angry girl who took drugs to cope with the shitty circumstances in her life. You haven't been that person for six years now, Tara, and it doesn't matter what happened today at Jackson's office. The girl that Brynn is so bitter and angry at is not the sober, responsible, independent woman you've become. And I'm pretty sure *that's* the woman Jackson wants in his life."

Everything Katrina said struck a chord in Tara and calmed the chaos that had been swirling inside of her since leaving Jackson's office. She felt more in control, more . . . like herself. Katrina was right. She couldn't spend the rest of her life living in the past, not if she wanted the kind of future she'd always hoped for and dreamed about. A future that included Jackson in every aspect of her life—if she had her way.

She'd talk to him and put her heart in his hands. What happened next was up to him.

Chapter Fourteen

I T TOOK JACKSON some time after his phone call had ended, and a whole lot of patience, to find out where Tara had gone after leaving his office. Once that business had been concluded, he'd gone straight to Walter's office to see if the other man could sit in on the three o'clock meeting Jackson had scheduled with a client. He'd been honest about his reasons for needing to leave, and thank God Walter had not only agreed to handle the appointment but had let Jackson know just how much he liked Tara, and he promised to talk to Brynn and make it clear that kind of attack wasn't welcome in the office.

Jackson couldn't have been more relieved or grateful for the other man's support. Then again, Walter, being a family man, was well aware of how bad Jackson's previous marriage had been and just how long it had taken him to recover from Collette's betrayal. Walter's parting words to Jackson had been,

Every man needs a good woman by his side, so don't let Tara slip through your fingers.

He refused to let that happen, and the first order of business was telling Tara how he felt about her. That there wasn't one thing—her past especially—that would keep him from loving her. Or being with her.

She didn't answer any of the text messages that he sent, so he drove to the most likely place he thought he'd find her—her house. But when he arrived, she wasn't there. His second guess had him picking up his cell phone and making a call to Clay so he didn't run around on a wild goose chase trying to locate her.

"You looking for Tara?" Clay answered the phone without a friendly greeting, his voice gruff and direct.

"Yes." Judging by Clay's brusque question, Jackson's brother knew something was going on, and he pressed him for answers. "How did you know? Is she at the bar?"

"No." Clay's voice remained cool as an iceberg. "Mason called to tell me that she came by Inked and that you did something to upset her."

Jackson pinched the bridge of his nose between his fingers. He knew *he* hadn't caused her to run. The situation had. But he wasn't going to argue the point with his twin. "Is she still there?"

"That all depends on why you want to see her."

Jesus Christ. He didn't have time for this shit and decided to be blunt. "To tell her I love her," Jackson replied, unable to conceal the frustration vibrating in his voice. "Is that a good enough reason?"

Clay was quiet for a long moment, then finally answered, sounding much less terse and more understanding. "Yeah, I suppose it is."

"So that means I have permission to see her?" Jackson asked sarcastically.

"From me, yes." There was a definite smirk in Clay's voice. "But good luck getting past Mason."

"Trust me, I can handle Mason," Jackson replied as he started driving toward Inked, anxious to see Tara and finally set things right between them.

"I do believe you can," Clay said with humor. He paused for a minute, then Jackson heard him release a deep breath before he added more seriously, "I know it was a rough few weeks when we first met, but I want you to know that I'm glad you contacted us and that you're a part of our family."

Jackson turned right on a street that led to the tattoo shop and felt his chest tighten with gratitude at his brother's confession. Six weeks ago, he wasn't sure he'd ever get to this point with his siblings, and was thankful to finally have their respect and acceptance. It's all he'd ever wanted from them.

"Thanks," Jackson said. "Me, too."

"And you're probably the best thing that has ever happened to Tara, so don't fuck it up."

Jackson chuckled, completely unoffended by Clay's threat. "She's the best thing that's ever happened to *me*, and I swear I'm going to do everything in my power to make her happy."

"Good," Clay said succinctly. "Then we should be

absolutely fine."

They ended the call, and a few minutes later he arrived at Inked, had the car parked, and strode determinedly into the shop. Mason was standing at the front counter, and he lifted a challenging brow as Jackson approached. Oh, yeah, this guy wasn't going to make any of this easy on him.

"Where is she?" he asked, far more politely than the demand he forced back down his throat.

"Who?" Mason asked, clearly feigning innocence.

Yeah, total asshole. "Tara. I know she's here, Mason."

His brother crossed his tattooed arms over his chest, not giving Jackson an inch. "What if she doesn't want to see you?"

"Did she say that?" he shot back.

"She didn't have to." Mason gave a careless, one-shoulder shrug. "She came in here crying and upset. What did you do to her?"

"I didn't do *anything* to her," he said through gritted teeth. "Not that it's any of your fucking business."

Mason arched a skeptical brow, but an accompanying smirk lifted his mouth, as if he liked the fact that Jackson had challenged him right back. "Yeah, well, it didn't look that way to me."

Jackson's aggravation rose another notch. "You know what, Mason? You're being a dick right now. You do realize that, don't you?"

The cocky bastard *grinned.* "Yeah, that's kind of how brothers are."

It was the first time Mason had referred to them as *brothers*. Realizing Jackson had cracked the toughest nut in the family—so to speak—made him feel as though he'd just gained entrance into a secret society. But this was even better, because it was everything he'd ever wanted and hoped for.

Mason relaxed his stance, a glint of amusement in his gaze. "Clay already called and told me that you were on your way and not to be a *dick* because you love Tara."

Jackson didn't know what he was more annoyed at. The fact that Mason had been jerking his chain from the moment he'd entered Inked or that Clay had revealed how Jackson felt about Tara. "Jesus, is nothing private?"

"Not between siblings," Mason told him. "Get used to it."

It was another subtle reference to being part of the Kincaid family, and probably the closest Jackson was going to get to any kind of acknowledgement from this particular brother. "If you don't let me talk to her, everyone in the goddamn city is going to know that I love Tara before she does!"

Finally, Mason took pity on him and jerked his head toward his office. "She's in there talking to Katrina. And I can guarantee that if you did anything stupid to Tara, Katrina will rip your nuts off."

Jackson wasn't sure if Mason was joking or not. "I find it hard to believe that your wife is more deranged than you."

Mason laughed, as if Jackson had just compliment-ed him. "Don't say I didn't warn you."

Done sparring with Mason, Jackson strode over to the office. Just as he reached for the doorknob—*no, he wasn't going to knock and announce himself and risk Tara refusing to see him*—the door swung open. Katrina came to an abrupt stop right in front of him, and Jackson resisted the urge to cup his hands over his balls to protect them, *just in case.*

"I want to talk to Tara." He wasn't asking permis-sion. His need to see her, *right now*, his feelings nonnegotiable.

"Okay," Katrina replied easily, then slid past him to leave the office, while Tara was still inside.

Well, that was easier than expected, Jackson thought.

He entered the room, then closed and locked the door behind him because he wanted privacy and no interruptions. He studied Tara a moment to gauge her emotions. She twisted her hands in front of her, and her eyes were wide as she stared back at him. He returned her gaze, but try as he might, Jackson wasn't able to pinpoint the emotions there.

He couldn't figure out where he currently stood with her, but that was fine, because before they left this office, she was going to know exactly where *she* stood with *him.*

Never taking his gaze off hers, he slowly moved toward her, closing the distance between them.

She swallowed hard and shifted anxiously on her feet as she watched his approach, that pretty dress of hers fluttering around her legs. "Jackson . . ."

He reached her the same moment she said his name, and he pressed his fingers over her lips, cutting off anything she'd been about to say. "Do not say a goddamn word," he said gruffly, refusing to give her any kind of possible opportunity to reject him. "Not until I'm done talking to you."

She just blinked up at him with those gorgeous blue eyes, silently complying, and it was so difficult to ignore just how soft and warm her mouth felt. It also took extreme effort not to replace his fingers with his lips on hers and kiss her until she melted against him and all those fears that had prompted her to bolt in the first place drifted away. Until there was just the two of them and none of this tension remained.

"I just need you to listen to me, okay?" he said in a gentler tone.

She nodded, and he moved his hand away, focusing on the reason he was here. "I love you, Tara," he said, watching the wonder and awe that shifted across her features. "I love everything single thing about you. From the moment I walked into the bar, I was drawn to you, and it didn't take me long to figure out why."

She stepped closer and settled a hand on his chest, right over his beating heart. "Tell me," she whispered.

He placed his palm over hers and searched her up-turned face, reveling in the open, receptive way her gaze held his. He didn't know what had prompted this change, but he took full advantage. "Because you're the other half of me that I've been waiting to find and the only woman who has ever made me feel whole and complete. I spent my entire life feeling like I wasn't a part of my own family, and years searching for that one place I belonged. And I found it, right here with you, and I hope to God you feel the same way."

Happy tears sparkled in her eyes. "I do. I love you, Jackson. So much it scares me."

He groaned in relief at her declaration, and sheer joy filled him to overflowing. "Sweetheart, there's no reason to be afraid. Ever. I'll always be here for you." It was a promise he intended to keep forever.

"I know. And I'm so sorry about what happened today at your office."

"You have no reason to apologize. You didn't do anything wrong. Brynn's reaction was the problem. Not you."

She let out a long breath. "I realize that now."

"Good. You can't let your past mistakes and actions define who you are now. You're a courageous woman who had the strength to make a better life for herself, despite the odds against you. *That's* the woman I want to marry."

"Marry?" she asked, her voice high-pitched and shocked.

"Yeah, marry." Grinning at her, he cupped her face in his hands and brushed his thumbs gently over her soft cheeks. "Will you be my wife, Tara Kent? You're the woman I adore and love and the only person I want to spend the rest of my life with. I want to protect you, cherish you, and make you mine.

Forever."

"Yes," she breathed, and gave him a radiant smile. "You make me happier than I ever believed possible. I've been through the struggle, and *you're* the happy ending to my story."

"Thank fuck," he said, and brought her mouth up to his, kissing her slow and sweet at first, which quickly escalated to hot, deep, and demanding. God, this woman was his everything, and he planned to spend every single day making sure she knew it, too.

After a while, he lifted his mouth from hers, and his lips quirked with a sinful grin as he looked into her desire-filled eyes. "You know, I ought to put you over my knee and spank you for running out on me and putting me through hell."

She bit her bottom lip, as if holding back a smile of her own. "Yes, I was very, very bad, and you should take me home right now and punish me."

Jesus. He grabbed her hand and pulled her toward the office door. She didn't have to tell him twice, not when he knew exactly what she both wanted and needed. And he intended to provide her with everything. Always.

Epilogue

J ACKSON WAS GOING to be an uncle. The thought made him grin as he walked into the hospital waiting room holding Tara's hand and met up with the rest of the Kincaid clan waiting for Clay and Samantha's baby to arrive. The past few months had been exciting ones. Two weddings—Levi and Sarah, then Jackson and Tara—and now the first baby being born into the family.

"Any news on baby Charlotte?" he asked, glancing at his two brothers.

"Not yet," Levi said from where he sat on a tweed chair with his wife, Sarah, by his side. The two of them had recently announced that she was pregnant, too, and they couldn't be more thrilled. "Samantha's going on six hours of labor, so hopefully soon."

Jackson smirked and didn't miss the opportunity to goad his sibling. "So, then we already know that Charlotte is going to be stubborn like her uncle

Mason, right?"

The girls laughed in agreement and Mason flipped him off. "You just wait. She's going to love her uncle Mason best. I'm going to be the cool uncle in the family."

"Don't worry, Jackson," Katrina chimed in, her gaze suddenly taking on a mischievous glint, even as she moved closer to Mason and slid her hand into his. "There's another little niece or nephew on the way, and I'll make sure he or she loves each uncle equally. No playing favorites."

Mason frowned at Katrina in confusion. "What are you talking about?"

Katrina suddenly gave Mason the sweetest, softest smile as she glanced up at him in adoration. "You're going to be a daddy."

The startled look that passed over Mason features was comical as realization struck. "Ho-ly fuck," he said in awe. "We're having a *baby*?" he asked in disbelief, as everyone else watched as the emotional moment played out between the couple.

Katrina slowly nodded. "Yeah, we are," she said, her voice filled with happiness. "That's why I've been nauseous for the past few weeks. It wasn't the flu after all."

Mason wrapped his wife in a huge, exuberant hug. "I can't believe we're having a fucking baby!" He released her and shook his head, still seemingly in shock. "How did it happen? We weren't even trying to get pregnant."

"It must have been that super sperm of yours," she said with a laugh.

"Oh, hell *yeah*," he said, and sealed his lips over Katrina's in a hot, passionate kiss that conveyed exactly how he felt about his wife and the new addition to their family they were going to have.

"Jesus, Mason," Levi said when the embrace went on a bit too long. "Get a goddamn room already."

"Screw you guys," Mason said, though he was beaming with pride. "My wife is having a fucking baby and I'll kiss her if I want to."

While Tara and Sarah fussed over Katrina, Jackson stepped up to his brother and shook his hand, their strong grip expressing the mutual respect they'd developed for each other as siblings. "Congratulations, Mason. I'm happy for you."

"Thanks, man."

The doors to the delivery area opened, and Clay burst through, a huge, elated smile on his face. "Charlotte is finally here," he announced, excitement infusing his voice. "She's healthy and beautiful, and Samantha and the baby are doing great."

"When can we see them?" Tara asked anxiously.

"I can take you guys in, two at a time, so her room doesn't get too crowded and Samantha doesn't feel overwhelmed."

Mason stepped forward, his hand in Katrina's. "Charlotte's favorite uncle gets to go first."

Clay just rolled his eyes. "Yeah, sure," he said, humoring his brother.

Everyone had a chance to visit mother and baby, and when it was Jackson and Tara's turn to head into the private room, Tara went straight for Samantha and the infant in her arms, while he hung back with his brother, watching the two women as they cooed over the squirming baby.

Jackson lightly slapped his twin brother on the back, grateful to be a part of this special moment. "Congratulations, Clay. You're a very lucky man."

"I know." Clay grinned at him, his gaze sliding to Tara. "So are you."

Jackson nodded in agreement. He was fortunate in so many ways, but the two things that mattered the most were having Tara as his wife and being a part of this family he'd been separated from at birth. Now, he couldn't imagine his life without either.

He glanced across the room and watched as Tara picked up Charlotte and held the infant in her arms. The look on Tara's face was so gentle, and he didn't miss the yearning he saw there, too. It caused his chest to expand with love, and it made him want to give her everything she'd ever wanted, including a baby of her own.

Once their time was up, he walked hand in hand with Tara out to his car.

She let out a soft sigh and glanced his way. "I can't believe that Katrina and Mason are having a baby, too," she said, her tone wistful.

"I know," he agreed as they came to a stop on the passenger side of his Porsche. He leaned in close and skimmed his lips against her neck and smiled as she shivered in response. "I'm feeling kind of left out. Want to go home and make a baby, Mrs. Kincaid?"

God, he loved the way that sounded. Before he'd married Tara, he'd had his last name legally changed back to Kincaid, with the support and approval of all three of his brothers—the ultimate form of acceptance into this family where he belonged.

Tara pulled back to search his gaze, the hope in her eyes shining bright. "Are you serious? You're ready to have kids?"

He gently tucked a silky strand of hair away from her cheek. "I've been ready to have a baby with you since the day we got married, and there's nothing more I want than to have a family with you. *Our* family."

"I want that, too," she whispered. "So much."

He touched his lips to hers and grinned. "Then let's go make it happen."

Thanks for reading!

Carly and Erika's newest books:
A Dare Crossover Series
Go HERE for info
carlyphillips.com/books/just-a-little-hookup

For Book News:
SIGN UP for Carly's Newsletter:
carlyphillips.com/CPNewsletter
SIGN UP for Erika's Newsletter:
https://geni.us/ErikaWildeNewsletter

Carly Phillips and Erika Wilde Booklist

A Dare Crossover Series
Just A Little Hookup (and more coming …)

Dirty Sexy Series
Dirty Sexy Saint
Dirty Sexy Inked
Dirty Sexy Cuffed
Dirty Sexy Sinner

Book Boyfriend Series
Big Shot
Faking It
Well Built
Rock Solid

The Boyfriend Experience

About the Authors

CARLY PHILLIPS is the bestselling author of over eighty sexy contemporary romances featuring hot men, strong women, and the emotionally compelling stories her readers have come to expect and love. She is happily married to her college sweetheart and the mother of two adult daughters and their crazy dogs. She loves social media and is always around to interact with her readers. You can find out more and get two free books at www.carlyphillips.com.

ERIKA WILDE is the author of the sexy Marriage Diaries series and The Players Club series. She lives in Oregon with her husband and two daughters, and when she's not writing you can find her exploring the beautiful Pacific Northwest. For more information on her upcoming releases, please visit website at www.erikawilde.com.